From a fine gold chain, a gemstone glowed with deep green fire.

Mary had never seen anything like it, and she hardly knew what to say.

"Oh, Walter—this is far too fine."

"Not at all. I picked out the stone and they set it just for you—that's what took so long. Here, I'll help you put it on."

Walter's fingers touched the nape of her neck when he fastened the clasp, and Mary shivered at the unexpected sensation.

Embarrassed, she went into the hall and stood before the mirror. The square-cut emerald brought out the green in her eyes and even added a touch of elegance to her denim jumper.

"It is a lovely necklace," she said, meaning it.

Walter smiled with pleasure. "It looks great on you, too. The stone is genuine—it came with papers."

"I've never had any jewelry with my birthstone," Mary said.

"Then it's time you did. I thought of your eyes the minute I saw this—I knew it would match them."

"I can't accept a gift like this," Mary began. She almost finished the sentence with "from someone I'm not engaged to marry," but stopped short.

Walter stood behind Mary with his hands on top of her shoulders, then bent to kiss the nape of her neck. Surprised, Mary shivered. Flustered, she turned from the mirror and into Walter's arms, where he held her close for what seemed a very long time.

D1115064

KAY CORNELIUS lives in Huntsville, Alabama, near the scenic areas described in *Mary's Choice*. She and her husband, Don, have two grown children and four growing grandchildren. They enjoy attending Elderhostels and serve as volunteer defensive driving instructors. Kay teaches the senior women's Bible study class in her church and likes to knit.

Books by Kay Cornelius

HEARTSONG PRESENTS
HP 60—More than Conquerors
HP 87—Sign of the Bow
HP 91—Sign of the Eagle
HP 95—Sign of the Dove
HP130—A Matter of Security
HP135—Sign of the Spirit
HP206—Politically Correct
HP561—Toni's Vow
HP577—Anita's Choice

Don't miss out on any of our super romances. Write to us at the following address for information on our newest releases and club information.

Heartsong Presents Readers' Service
PO Box 719
Uhrichsville, OH 44683

Or visit www.heartsongpresents.com

Mary's Choice

Kay Cornelius

Heartsong Presents

In loving memory of my grandmother, Mary Griggs Whitehead ("Mother Mary" to all who knew her), and my mother, "Pinkie" Whitehead Oldham, women whose lives reflected what they told me: "Pretty is as pretty does."

A note from the Author:
I love to hear from my readers! You may correspond with me by writing:

Kay Cornelius
Author Relations
PO Box 719
Uhrichsville, OH 44683

ISBN 1-59310-139-2

MARY'S CHOICE

Copyright © 2004 by Kay Cornelius. All rights reserved. Except for use in any review, the reproduction or utilization of this work in whole or in part in any form by any electronic, mechanical, or other means, now known or hereafter invented, is forbidden without the permission of Heartsong Presents, an imprint of Barbour Publishing, Inc., PO Box 719, Uhrichsville, Ohio 44683.

Our mission is to publish and distribute inspirational products offering exceptional value and biblical encouragement to the masses.

All Scripture quotations are taken from the HOLY BIBLE, NEW INTERNATIONAL VERSION ®. NIV®. Copyright © 1973, 1978, 1984 by International Bible Society. Used by permission of Zondervan Publishing House. All rights reserved.

All of the characters and events in this book are fictitious. Any resemblance to actual persons, living or dead, or to actual events is purely coincidental.

PRINTED IN THE U.S.A.

Or check out our Web site at www.heartsongpresents.com

one

"Happy birthday, Miss Mary!" eighteen first-graders shouted more or less in unison when Mary Oliver entered her classroom at two o'clock on the third Friday in May.

Summoned to the principal's office fifteen minutes earlier, Mary had told Ann Ward, her student teacher, she couldn't imagine what Mrs. Martin wanted that couldn't wait until school was out. "Hold down the fort—I should be back soon."

Now Mary stood in shocked surprise and looked around. Dark pink crepe paper streamers and pink and white balloons decorated the room, and HAPPY BIRTHDAY TO OUR TEACHER was written in large letters on the chalkboard. The top of Mary's desk had been cleared to make room for a sheet cake on which thirty candles blazed. Smiling broadly, blond student teacher Ann Ward and brunette room mother Katie Pierce flanked the cake.

"Blow out the candles, Miss Mary!" Tommy Pierce shouted.

"Then she can see the presents and we can have cake," added his twin sister, Tammy.

Mary looked from the children crowding around her to the women beside the desk and shook her head. "I didn't think anyone knew it was my birthday."

"We thought you deserved to be included in the birthday calendar, too," Katie Pierce said. "Mrs. Martin agreed, and Miss Ward helped us."

"Hurry, Miss Mary! Blow out the candles before the cake burns up," Lance Hastings said.

"She has to make a wish first," Tammy Pierce said.

"I can't think of a thing to wish for," Mary said.

"You could wish for a husman, Miss Mary," Juanita Sanchez suggested.

5

"Husband," Mary corrected as a chorus of little voices joined to ask her to wish for a man. "I'd rather think of something nice for all of you instead," Mary said.

"That's right, if Miss Mary wanted a husman, she'd already have one," Jackie Tate declared.

Mary's last shred of composure crumbled, and she laughed so hard she could scarcely take a deep breath.

"It's your birthday, so you can have three tries," Juanita Sanchez said when Mary's first effort extinguished only a few candles.

"I think you just made a new birthday rule," Katie Pierce said.

With a second breath, Mary blew out most of the remaining candles, and when her third attempt extinguished the rest, the children cheered and applauded.

"That means Miss Mary can have three husbands," Jackie Tate declared.

Katie Pierce smiled at the child. "One at a time, of course."

After having cake, the children gathered around Mary in the story area and watched her examine the two-page books each had made. All bore the hand-printed heading "My Teacher" and the student's picture of Mary. The second page, written using the classroom computer, contained an individual "story" about their teacher.

"What a fine job you all did!" Mary exclaimed as she held up each one for inspection. In fact, many of the boys and girls had gone out of their way to create a realistic portrait, complete with impossibly large green eyes. Some had given her two-toned red and yellow hair in an effort to capture Mary's unique strawberry blond shade. Some showed her with tiny feet and hands and a big head, while one budding Rembrandt depicted Mary as a snowman in a blue dress. Mary suspected they'd had more than a little help from their student teacher, who had spent several afternoons with the class during the past week while Mary held year-end parent conferences.

The students' stories contained sentiments such as "I like

my teacher," "Miss Mary helps me," and "I love her."

Mary's eyes brimmed with sudden tears. She loved "her" children, too, more than they could ever know. "Thank you all for making this birthday very special."

"Your students really love you," Ann Ward said a few minutes later when the school day ended. "I hope I can be half the teacher you are."

You're already half my size. The flippant words almost slipped out. Mary judged Ann Ward to be a perfect size eight, in contrast to her own sixteen petite dress size.

"Thanks, Ann. My best advice to you is to follow the lead of the Master Teacher. If you can do that, you can't go wrong."

Ann nodded. "That's exactly what Jason said when I told him I wanted to be a teacher."

"Jason? I don't believe you've mentioned him."

"Jason Abbott—he's an older cousin. I haven't seen him since I was a college freshman, but I just found out he's coming to Rockdale soon."

Katie Pierce had been listening to their conversation and addressed Ann. "I had no idea you were related to Jason Abbott. He's been called to be my church's associate pastor."

"Toni Trent mentioned Community Church was adding to the staff," Mary said. "She'll be glad to know he's from a good family."

Ann smiled. "On my mother's side, anyway. When you get to know him, I'm sure you'll like him."

"Pastor Hurley can't wait for him to get here and start some new programs."

"My mother said Jason feels the same way," Ann said. "I'm sorry to be leaving town just as he's about to arrive."

When the classroom had been restored to order, Ann helped Mary take her students' gifts and the remaining birthday cake to her car.

"You'll probably have another birthday cake waiting when you get home," Ann said.

"I doubt it. My father and I are having dinner at the country club tonight, and that will be it."

"You don't have any other family around here?"

Mary opened the trunk of her aging Toyota, the first car she'd bought with her own money, and moved several book-filled plastic crates to make room for her students' birthday books. "Not really. The Olivers have scattered all over the map. About the only time we see them is on Decoration Day, when we tend the family cemetery on Memorial Day week-end. That reminds me—I still have a few more calls to make."

"You're in charge, I suppose?"

Mary shrugged. "Not officially, but I try to remind everyone."

"Dad's aunt Frances did such things in our family. She never married." Ann stopped suddenly, and Mary silently supplied *either*. Obviously, Ann assumed being single auto-matically made Mary the family record keeper.

"Thank you for helping with my party," Mary said. "The children and I will miss you."

Ann stepped back as Mary slammed the trunk shut. "I know I'm out of line to say this, but I think it's a shame you haven't married and had your own children. You'd make such a good mother."

Mary had heard similar statements before, and she gave Ann her stock answer. "I love being first-graders' school-hours mother. That's enough for me."

≈

She thought she sounded convincing, but Ann's comment echoed in her mind on her drive home. *You'd make such a good mother.*

Mary usually dismissed such statements without a second thought. Since feeling God's call in her teens to teach, Mary had presumed she would remain single.

Not that I ever had much choice. Overweight from childhood, Mary had avoided being hurt by rejecting the few men who didn't mind being seen with her. She had settled into a com-fortable routine, working with children and making a home for her father.

"Home" was a turreted Victorian built by her great-grandfather Hugh Oliver. "A real Southern showplace," the pages of a prestigious magazine featuring Alabama homes had described it. Mary had no illusions about it, however. The house tended to be cold in the winter and, despite strategically placed window air conditioners and fans in the high ceilings, it could also be hot in the summer.

Mary turned into the driveway and went around to the back where the original carriage house now served as a two-car garage and storage for the Olivers' lawnmower and gardening tools. She noted the absence of her father's stately black sedan. Judge Wayne Oliver had been hearing cases all week, and he would probably stay at the Rock County Courthouse until well after five in an effort to clear the current docket.

Mary put her birthday gift books on the dining room table. In the kitchen she scraped the lettering from the icing, double-wrapped the leftover cake in foil, and put it in the freezer. Later she could bring it out and share it with her father as an end-of-school cake. On the thirtieth anniversary of his daughter's birth, Wayne Oliver needed no more reminders of the day that also marked his wife's death.

Mary recalled how, when she was four, she had realized everyone else in her world had a real mother, while all she had was a picture of a pretty young woman in a white dress.

"Aunt Janie, where is my mother?" Mary had asked the black woman who had helped raise her mother and was now doing the same for her.

"Miss Grace be in heaven, Miss Mary. She loved the Lord, and His angels done took her right up there."

At the time, Mary made no connection between her birth and her mother's death, but when she was six, her aunt Lucy Austin had taken Mary to her first Decoration Day. Sylvia, Aunt Lucy's ten-year-old daughter, took Mary aside and showed her the family's burial plot.

"That's your mama's grave." Sylvia then read the inscription aloud.

"May 21—that's my birthday," Mary said.

"I heard my mama say your mama died 'cause something busted inside of her when you were born. If it hadn't been for you, Aunt Grace would still be alive 'stead of lyin' here under all this dirt."

That evening, Mary had climbed into Aunt Janie's ample lap and sobbed inconsolably.

"What's de matter, chile?"

"Sylvie Austin told me I killed my mother," she said between sobs.

"You never killed nobody, chile. Don't pay no attention to that gal, 'cause she don't have a brain in her head. You was born 'cause God wanted you here on earth, and He took Miss Grace to heaven 'cause He needed her there. It don't do to try to say why God does what He does. Come on, darlin'—quit cryin' and Aunt Janie'll give you a hunk of the chocolate cake I made for you this mornin'."

The cake tasted good and Mary felt better, at least for the moment. Whenever Mary got hurt or had a problem, Aunt Janie was always there with something good to eat. As a result, Mary had gone from toddler "baby fat" to a childhood of wearing hard-to-find chubby-size clothing. She began her painful teen years in ill-fitting women's plus-sizes.

Fatty, fatty, two by four. . .
Can't get through the kitchen door. . .

The taunting had started early and continued long after Mary had learned to close her ears to it. At a church camp in her fifteenth summer, the leader had taken Mary aside and used Scriptures to show her how much the Creator God loved her, just as she was, just as she had been made.

"There is no such thing as an ugly body to God. He loves you *in* your body. His grace covers everything you see as a fault, just as His blood covered your sins when you accepted Jesus as your Lord and Savior."

From that day, Mary's attitude changed, not only about the way she looked but also about everything in her life. When she was no longer the center of all her thoughts, Mary found others who needed to know the peace she had found in accepting God's grace. One such person, Toni Schmidt, had recently returned to Rockdale and was now Mary's best friend.

Once Mary understood what she had allowed food to become, she had begun to lose weight by learning to eat only when she was physically hungry. By popular standards, she was still overweight when she graduated from college, but Dr. Mason, who had tended two generations of Austins and Olivers, wasn't concerned.

"You're a healthy young woman. Get married and have lots of babies. Don't even think about trying to diet yourself to death."

Mary spread out the portraits the students had made of her and thought of the advice Dr. Mason had delivered almost a decade ago.

"Marriage isn't in the picture for me," Mary had told the doctor. Then, she had automatically dismissed all thought of marriage; now, she wasn't so sure.

"Mary—I'm home. Where are you?"

Judge Oliver came in through the kitchen, and Mary heard him put his briefcase on a table in the front hall.

"In the dining room. Come see what my students did."

Wayne Oliver shrugged out of his suit jacket and hung it on the antique walnut hall tree. Much taller than his daughter, he had a large frame which carried only a few more pounds than it had in his football playing years at the University of Alabama. Like his daughter, the judge had the kind of round, high-cheekboned face which looked youthful even past middle age. His eyes were the same unusual shade of green as Mary's, while his close-cropped salt-and-pepper hair contrasted with his daughter's strawberry blond bob.

"I take it your class did something good?"

"With my student teacher's help. Every child in the class made a book for me."

Wayne Oliver's stern countenance, befitting his position as

a judge, softened when he viewed the pictures. "Quite a collection of portraits," he said after a moment. "Looks like you have a pretty good crop of kids this year."

"As usual," Mary said.

Her father glanced at his wristwatch. "We have reservations at the country club for six-thirty. We'll leave about six. Put on something nice."

Mary watched her father walk away, humming as he all but skipped up the stairs. He had been acting a bit strange lately. Usually she had to nag him to buy clothes, but a few weeks ago he had gone to Birmingham on his own and returned with a new suit and several casual shirts and slacks. Last weekend he had disappeared for hours with no explanation. And, oddest and most telling of all, he smiled a lot more these days.

He's up to something, all right—I wonder what.

two

"You look very handsome in your new suit," Mary said when her father came down the stairs promptly at six.

He glanced at it as if he hadn't noticed what he was wearing. "Do I? Thanks."

"Why are we going so early?" Mary asked as they left the house.

"You'll see."

Instead of turning right, toward Rockdale Country Club, Wayne Oliver turned left toward town. He circled the courthouse and turned right, then right again.

Her father stopped the car in front of 210 Maple Street, a house she knew well. Toni Schmidt had lived there as a teenager after Evelyn Trent became her legal guardian, and again when she'd returned to town a couple of years ago to take over Evelyn's job. Toni had moved out after marrying Evelyn's brother last year, and Evelyn had recently returned to town after a second round of extensive traveling.

"I'll be right back," her father said.

While he mounted the porch steps and rang the doorbell, Mary got into the back seat to allow Evelyn to sit up front. Apparently Wayne Oliver, who had avoided going out with women as long as Mary could remember, had invited Evelyn, the retired director of the Rockdale office of the Department of Human Resources, to accompany them to the country club. Not an official date, perhaps, but close.

Evelyn appeared at the door, trim and stylish in a long navy blue sheath. Her pearl necklace and earrings accented her blue eyes, silver-white hair, and smooth ivory skin. *This isn't the first time they've gone out*, Mary guessed, but they must have kept it under wraps, because she hadn't heard even a whisper about it—and with all the busybodies and gossips in Rockdale, she most certainly would have.

Wayne Oliver offered Evelyn his arm, and they came down the steps looking like an elegant couple in an advertisement for something extravagantly expensive. A lump rose in Mary's throat as she saw how much they already looked as if they belonged together.

"Hello, Mary," Evelyn said when she had been installed in the front seat. "How's school? I suppose you're counting the days to the end of the term."

"In a way, but it's a bittersweet time. I've had really fine children this year, and I hate to lose them."

"I hear that every year," her father said. "One of these days, Mary's bound to have a class full of little stinkers."

"If so, I'm sure she'll turn them around. She certainly did a great job with my nephew."

"Josh was never a bad child—he just missed his mother. Once Toni came into his life, he blossomed."

"Speaking of Toni, she and David will be there tonight," Wayne Oliver said.

Evelyn half turned to address Mary. "Toni has certainly made a wonderful stepmother for my brother's children."

"When I remanded Toni Schmidt to your custody all those years ago, I never imagined where it would lead," the judge observed.

"Neither did I," Evelyn agreed. "The Lord indeed moves in mysterious ways."

❧

Mary expected they would sit in the main dining room, but the hostess told him some of his guests were already waiting in the Rock Room.

Lloyd Hastings, husband of long-time Rockdale Mayor Margaret Hastings; Randall Bell, retired lawyer and lifelong friend of Wayne Oliver; and Realtor Walter Chance stood as Judge Oliver's party approached the large, round table in the private dining room.

Mary was surprised to see Walter Chance, a high school classmate with whom she'd worked on their tenth reunion. His perennial smile and brick-red hair made him look somewhat clownlike at first glance, but no one could deny he was serious about reviving his family's real estate business.

Walter smiled widely and pulled out the chair next to his for Mary. "That's a pretty dress."

"Thanks, Walter."

"Hello, Mary, Evelyn," said Margaret Hastings when they were seated. "You both look stunning."

Mary accepted the compliment, although she suspected it was intended more for Evelyn. Mary knew her green crepe dress—bought on sale for more than she cared to admit—set off her green eyes and ivory skin, and the long lines of the jacket added an illusion of height and made her seem pounds lighter. But *stunning* was not the word Mary thought anyone else would likely use.

"Red is definitely your color, Margaret," Evelyn observed.

"Thanks," said the mayor. "Look, here comes Toni Trent. I'm glad she didn't wear her hot pink dress tonight. When we wind up being seated together, those colors clash badly."

Mary turned to see Toni, wearing a light blue dress under a darker blue jacket, enter with David Trent, Evelyn's brother.

Once again the men stood, and Toni took the chair to Mary's left. "It's been too long since we got together."

Mary still considered Toni to be her best friend, but since Toni's marriage, they hadn't been as close. Being the last remaining single, never-married women in their Rockdale High School graduating class had given them a shared bond when Toni had come back to Rockdale to live, determined not to marry. However, after Mary saw David and Toni together, she wasn't surprised when they became engaged, and she rejoiced in her friend's happiness.

"Our colors blend well tonight," Margaret Hastings told Toni. "I'm glad you didn't wear your hot pink dress."

"I probably would have, but I can't get into it now."

Mary glanced at Toni and saw her waistline had thickened considerably since she'd last seen her. Toni didn't seem to be upset by the change—in fact, her face glowed with happiness.

"Is there something we should know?" Mary asked.

David took his wife's hand and smiled broadly. "Toni wanted to keep it quiet as long as possible, but we're expecting a baby in October."

"How wonderful!" Mary hugged her friend. "Do Josh and Mandy know?"

"Yes, but we asked them not to tell anyone for a while. They can't wait to have a little brother or sister."

"You don't know which?" asked Margaret.

"No. We'll take whatever the Lord sends us and rejoice," David said.

"That's a good attitude," Randall Bell said. "Just paint the nursery all-purpose white. That's what my daughter Joan did with both of hers."

Just then Dr. Vance Whitson, pastor of First Church, and his wife arrived.

"This is quite an occasion," Lloyd Hastings observed when the couple took the remaining seats. "As long as I've known Wayne Oliver, I believe this is his first dinner party. I suppose you're responsible, Mary."

She shook her head. "No—I didn't know anything about it until we got here."

"I think I know who assisted Judge Oliver." Margaret smiled at Evelyn, whose cheeks flushed becomingly.

"The judge wanted to surprise Mary, and I offered to help," Evelyn said.

Randall Bell, a long-time widower, smiled at Evelyn. "Excellent choice. Maybe you should start catering, now that you've retired."

"No thanks, Randall. I stay so busy now I really don't know when I ever had time to work."

Wayne Oliver tapped his glass with a spoon. "I'm glad you could all join us. Dr. Whitson, will you offer our thanks?"

A bit dazed, Mary bowed her head as her church's senior pastor provided a lengthy blessing for the food.

❧

Later, if anyone had asked about the menu that evening, Mary would have been hard-pressed to name even one dish. Walter Chance did his best to make entertaining small talk, while everyone at the table noticed the attention Wayne Oliver was paying Evelyn Trent, who sat beside him, blushing like a schoolgirl and laughing at his somewhat lame jokes.

This evening is about them, not me. Mary wanted her father to be happy, but seeing him and Evelyn together made her feel oddly alone. *He must have realized it would and invited Walter to keep me company.*

During dinner, conversation turned to rumors about changes coming to the town of Rockdale as outside interests sought to buy land or start new ventures.

"It's time we got together to decide how to deal with these things," Randall Bell said. "As much as some of us might want to, we can't stop changes from happening, but we ought to prepare to direct it for the good of everyone in Rockdale and Rock County."

Judge Oliver nodded in agreement. "Some of us have been considering what to do about this for some time—our mayor here, Newman Howell, Sam Roberts, and Dr. Endicott, to name a few. We agree it's time for everyone who's interested in managing Rockdale's growth to get together. Mayor Hastings has agreed to open the city council chambers next Tuesday night and serve as an ex officio chairman of a new organization to be known as the Rockdale Civic Improvement Association. Anyone who cares about what happens to Rockdale is invited to be a part of it."

"That sounds like a good idea," said Walter Chance.

"Be thinking about it. For the moment, there's a much more important item on the agenda," the judge said.

At the host's signal, the kitchen doors opened, and the headwaiter wheeled in a cart bearing a birthday cake. A buzz of conversation confirmed it was as much a surprise to the guests as to Mary.

Judge Oliver, who cheerfully admitted he couldn't carry a tune in a bucket, waved both hands in an attempt to direct a ragged rendition of the traditional happy birthday song.

Mary had no trouble looking surprised. Her face turned red, and although she wanted to slide out of sight beneath the table, she tried to smile. She was grateful someone had the good sense to put a single large candle on this cake, unlike the thirty small ones on her school cake.

The headwaiter stopped the cart beside Mary and stepped aside, and Toni tugged on her sleeve. "Stand up. You have to make a wish and blow out the candle."

With a strange feeling of déjà vu, Mary rose and blew out the oversized candle, bringing a round of applause.

Her father stood beside Mary and put his arm around her shoulders. "I don't know what my daughter wished for, but I hope she gets it. I'm proud of Mary, and it's time I told her so."

Mary hugged her father, too full of tears to speak, and when she sat down again and saw tears gleaming in Evelyn's eyes, she suspected the retired social worker had played a part in more than merely arranging the dinner.

The headwaiter cut a huge chunk of the cake for Mary, then his assistants moved in to serve everyone else.

"It's chocolate!" Mary exclaimed.

"I know that's your favorite. Your mother loved chocolate, too."

"Thank you. This is just what I wanted," Mary said, and they both understood she meant the sentiment, not the cake.

"You should have reminded us it was Mary's birthday," Margaret Hastings told Judge Oliver.

"That's right, Wayne. We would gladly have brought a gift if we'd known," Randall Bell said.

"I'm glad you didn't," Mary said.

Evelyn nodded. "I told your father you'd feel that way."

A few minutes later, when they went to freshen their

makeup, Mary took the opportunity to speak to Toni. "That's great news about you and David. I'd like to give you a baby shower this summer."

"Thanks. We have a room in our house we've always called the nursery, but we don't have a thing in it."

"Look at your calendar and come up with a date—a Friday night in July or August will probably work for everyone."

"Will you be in town all summer?" Toni asked.

"Yes. I hope to have time to vegetate for a change."

"That's what I'll do, if David has his way, but I want to work as long as I can. I'd rather stay home longer after the baby comes than to quit weeks before."

"As long as you feel well, I see no reason why you shouldn't keep working."

"That's what I told David. Besides, Evelyn has agreed to fill in while I'm on maternity leave, so my job will be in good hands."

Mary was silent for a moment. "Speaking of Evelyn, how long has my father been seeing her?"

"I don't know, but I think it's about time for them both."

"Lately my father has seemed rather preoccupied. Now I believe it's because of Evelyn."

"Do you approve?" Toni asked.

Mary shrugged. "I like Evelyn, but after all the years he's dodged well-meaning widows, it's strange to see him dating."

"David and I felt the same way about Evelyn at first, too. It should be interesting to see what happens."

❧

When the dinner ended and Walter Chance offered to take Mary home, she suspected her father had planned it that way.

"There are still a few hours left in your birthday," Walter said on the way to his car. "Maybe we should continue the celebration somewhere else."

Mary smiled. "In Rockdale? I don't know where that would be. Thanks, anyway."

Walter helped Mary into his sedan but made no move to

start the engine. He had parked beneath a bright security light, and Mary saw his expression was uncharacteristically serious when he turned to her.

"It really meant a lot for the judge to included me tonight. Since Mother's been gone, I've had to eat alone most nights."

Walter's mention of his mother made Mary feel uncomfortable. For years, Roberta Chance had done her best to make her only son into the kind of mama's boy no girl in her right mind would want to marry—and finding fault with anyone Walter showed even a slight interest in. Then a few months ago, Walter's mother had shocked Rockdale by eloping with a Georgia timber cruiser she'd known only a short time, leaving Walter in full control of the business his late father had started. Mrs. Chance's sudden departure had dumbfounded her son and set gossips' tongues wagging.

Although Mary privately thought it was probably the best thing that ever happened to Walter, she knew the sudden change in his life must have affected him deeply, and her sympathy was genuine. "I know this has been a difficult time. Where is your mother living?"

"Atlanta at the moment, but her husband travels all over the Southeast. There's no telling where they'll be next week."

"You're bound to miss her very much, but I'm glad to see you're getting on with your own life."

"I've been trying to. I'm glad you understand—most people around here don't."

Walter Chance was an old friend, and Mary couldn't help feeling sorry for him. "Everyone says you're doing wonders for Chance Realty."

Walter brightened. "I'm still working out some changes, but the business is doing well."

"Your father would be proud of you."

Walter grinned. "Your father sure must be proud of you, to throw you a dinner party like that."

"My birthday wasn't the only reason for it," Mary said. She meant the talk about forming a civic improvement association, but Walter apparently had another idea.

"I think the judge wanted to be seen with Miss Trent. Do you think they'll get married?"

The question startled Mary. "Can't they enjoy each other's company without assuming they're headed for the altar?"

"Not in Rockdale—you know that's the way it is around here. Anyway, I think they make a nice couple."

So did Mary, but she didn't care to discuss her father's personal life. "I'd like to go home. This has been a long day."

Walter was instantly contrite. "Of course you're tired after teaching all day. Forgive me for talking your ear off."

"You didn't—no harm done."

When they reached her home, Walter escorted Mary to her door. "I didn't know today was your birthday, but I intend to give you something, anyway."

"Please don't. Your friendship is gift enough."

Walter's eyes widened. "Really?"

Why did I say that? "We've been friends since kindergarten, I mean."

"We're not in kindergarten now." As if to prove it, Walter gave Mary an awkward hug.

She stammered in surprise. "I—I don't want you to give me anything. I mean it."

"And I mean what I say, too," Walter said cheerfully. "Good night, Mary."

She closed the door behind him and stood for a moment in the dark hallway. Moonlight streamed into the front windows, making everything seem somehow strange and unfamiliar.

Like this evening.

Mary believed her father was correct—Rockdale had resisted many outside forces for years, but change was inevitable. In fact, many such changes had probably already been set into motion.

And so it is with my father and me. It seems he's finally found someone to love.

Could Mary do the same? *Perhaps Rockdale isn't the only thing about to change.*

three

The last few days of the school year passed in a blur of reports and good-byes. Ann Ward, who was to graduate and move to Seattle that summer, repeated how much she'd learned from Mary.

"I hope you'll get to meet Jason soon," she added. "You two would get along great."

"I'm sure we would, if he's anything like you," Mary said, but she thought it unlikely their paths would cross. Jason Abbott would be at Community Church, and Mary attended First Church. *"And never the twain shall meet."*

With school out of the way, Mary completed plans for the annual Decoration Day. Mary and her father never knew exactly how many relatives would show up to tend the family graves on the last Sunday in May, but everyone would come to the Oliver house for a light supper on Sunday evening.

"It seems fewer people turn out every year," Wayne Oliver remarked when they saw the half dozen cars parked around the cemetery on Sunday afternoon. "This new generation doesn't seem to care about family traditions."

What new generation? Mary almost asked. She could count the relatives near her age on the fingers of one hand, and she was the only one who still lived in Rockdale.

The cemetery was situated on flat land at the top of Oliver Mountain, one of several ridges surrounding Rockdale. A stone fence surrounded the plot, and a hundred-year-old wrought iron gate marked the entrance. Many of the jumbled, weathered tombstones were shaded by oak, maple, and hickory tree, whose roots had caused cracks in several of the older stones. A spring-fed stream splashed on nearby rocks as it made its way down the mountain, and the soft wind sighed through the trees, the only sounds other than the songs of birds.

"This place is more beautiful every year," Mary remarked.

"And needs more attention. When I was here last week, I noticed the Austin headstones need cleaning. You can start there."

Mary glanced at her mother's great-great-grandparents' graves, among the oldest in the cemetery. "The headstones look newly cleaned."

"So they do. The question is, who did it?"

"I plead guilty, Judge Oliver," a male voice said.

Mary turned to the speaker, a well-built, dark-haired man with startling, deep blue eyes. He wore jeans and a battered red shirt with "Alabama Football" stenciled on the front. Mary hadn't seen him in at least ten years, but she recognized him instantly.

Todd Walker. A distant cousin on her mother's side of the family, five years older, and football star at the University of Alabama. Throughout her teen years, Mary had had a secret crush on Todd, who had scarcely known she existed. Even now, years later, he still made her heart beat a bit faster.

"Todd!" Wayne Oliver exclaimed. "I had no idea you were back in Alabama."

"I've been working in Birmingham for a couple of months. I looked at the calendar Friday and realized it was time for Decoration Day, so I threw a few tools in the truck and drove over this morning. I took the liberty of cleaning a few stones before anyone else arrived. I hope you don't mind."

"Not at all. They look almost like new."

Todd turned his attention to Mary. "I was hoping to see you today, Mary Oliver—or do you have a different last name now?"

Mary shook her head, feeling as tongue-tied in his presence as when she was a love-struck teenager. "No."

"You kids can catch up with each other while you work," Wayne Oliver said. "As you can see, there's much to be done."

When her father called her and Todd "kids," Mary winced.

She was thirty, and Todd had to be thirty-five. Granted, they weren't exactly dead with old age, but both were past being kids.

If Todd noticed her father's use of the term, he didn't show it. "Where would you like for us to start, sir?"

Us. Mary smiled inwardly at Todd's casual reference. In assuming he and Mary would work together, Todd made it sound as if they were a couple.

"Since you've already done the headstones, you might as well work in the Austin plot. There aren't many Austin kin left, and I doubt if any others will show up today."

"I see you came prepared," Todd said when her father left to greet a few late arrivals.

At first Mary thought he referred to the straw hat, blue jeans, and long-sleeved shirt salvaged from her father's wardrobe, then she realized he meant her heavy gloves and grass clippers. "I wear the gloves to weed and use the shears to trim places the lawnmower can't reach."

"Good idea." Todd spread out his hands, which were at least twice the size of Mary's, and, like hers, ringless. "The gloves obviously won't fit me, but I can use the clippers while you pull weeds."

They began to clear the area around the newly cleaned stones. " 'Warren Austin,' " Todd read from the headstone. "According to my mother's family tree, he's a 'way back grandfather.' "

"Mine, too. He was my great-great-great-grandfather."

"So what kin does that make us?" Todd asked.

"Fifth cousins, I believe. Or maybe we're first cousins, five times removed. I don't know much about genealogy."

"Neither do I. But I'm much more interested in learning about my roots now than when I was a kid."

So Todd noticed her father's comment, after all. Mary returned Todd's slight smile and resumed her work without saying anything.

After a moment, Todd spoke again. "I take it you stayed here in Rockdale?"

"Yes. I teach first grade at Rockdale Elementary."

"I'm not surprised. You're just right for a place like Rockdale."

As Todd spoke, a stubborn sheaf of Johnson grass Mary had been tugging at a long while suddenly yielded, and Mary sat down hard. Embarrassed, she spoke quickly. "I always thought you'd go off and do great things in some big city."

Todd laughed. "So did I, but right now I'm doing rather small things in Birmingham. It isn't exactly a metropolis, but I wanted to get back to Alabama."

"I heard you were living in California. You didn't like it?"

"The weather was great—other things weren't."

Todd's tone warned her to avoid personal questions, and Mary was glad when he asked about present-day Rockdale. "I hear it's on the verge of a lot of growth. How do you feel about that?"

"Everyone says change is inevitable, but I hope Rockdale won't try to grow just for the sake of growth. I like it just as it is now."

"Nothing stays the same forever. Organisms must grow and change or they'll die. The same thing applies to towns."

"That sounds like something from Sociology 101."

Todd smiled. "You caught me there. People in Alabama who remember me at all probably still think I'm a dumb jock. I didn't want the Olivers to think that, too."

Mary had never thought of Todd as lacking intelligence, but his concern seemed real. "I don't," Mary said, "and I'm sure my father doesn't, either. He played football, too, you know."

"I'd almost forgotten. I'm sure no one would ever call Judge Oliver 'dumb.'"

"Not to his face, at least." Mary stood and stretched. "I think we've done all we can here. I'm thirsty—it's time for a break."

Several workers were already gathered around the cooler, pouring lemonade from gallon jugs.

"This is great stuff," Todd said.

"Mary makes this every year," said Nancy Oliver. "The

lemonade and supper afterward are just bribes to get us here."

"Whatever works," Wayne Oliver said.

After a brief rest, Todd went to help Mary's father on the Oliver side. Although she had worn gloves, Mary found blisters forming on the thumb and index finger of her right hand, so she spent the rest of the afternoon cleaning headstones with Nancy.

By the time the sun went down behind Oliver Mountain, more than a dozen workers had trimmed around every grave and filled a number of trash bags with weeds, grass, and debris from the small cemetery. Satisfied with the result of their labors, Wayne Oliver thanked the participants for another successful Decoration Day and invited them to his home for supper.

"I hope you'll join us," Wayne told Todd as they left the cemetery.

"Sure. I can't miss the chance to see your wonderful house again," Todd said.

On their way back to town, Mary told her father she didn't recall ever seeing Todd Walker at their home. *As much as I admired him, I believe I would have remembered it.*

"Todd and his mother came to Decoration Day almost every year until she passed away. You must have been away at college the last few times they came together. Since Gladys died, Todd hasn't been back to Rockdale. Why do you ask?"

"No reason."

Mary had never told anyone how she felt about Todd Walker when she was growing up, and she saw no need to confess it to her father now.

The Decoration Day workers arrived at the Oliver house hot and tired. Mary brought minted iced tea to the long tables on one of the two screened-in porches, then returned to the kitchen for the platters of sandwiches and brownies she had made the day before.

Todd followed Mary into the kitchen and offered to help serve.

"You seem to know your way around a kitchen," she remarked a few minutes later.

"I've done my own cooking for years. It's become sort of a hobby."

Mary hesitated to say anything personal, but he had provided a good opening. "It sounds as if you live alone."

Todd directed his attention to removing the plastic wrap over a plate of deviled eggs. "Yes. I've had a few roommates, but they never worked out."

Were his roommates male or female? Mary was curious, but it was none of her business, so she kept silent.

"Leave the eggs on the counter so I can sprinkle them with paprika," she said after a few moments.

Todd watched Mary add the finishing touch to the deviled egg platter. "I remember seeing your housekeeper do that the last time I was here—I think she was called Aunt Janie. Does she still work for you?"

"Unfortunately, she died of a heart attack just before I graduated from college." The words were hard to say, even years later.

"Sorry. I know you were very close."

She was like a mother to me. I still miss her. Mary nodded. "You can take the eggs in now. I'll serve the brownies later."

"So you did all this by yourself?" Todd sounded impressed.

"Such as it is. We'd better get the eggs on the table so my father can bless the food."

While they ate, the relatives retold old stories and passed around information and pictures of absent family members. A motherless only child, Mary always enjoyed this annual opportunity to feel a connection with others who shared her heritage.

Todd sat beside Mary and seemed genuinely interested in each of the family stories. *Either he's having a good time or he's a good actor.*

Eventually, everyone moved to the front hall for long good-byes. Mary returned to the porch to find Todd Walker had already wrapped and refrigerated the few leftovers and was clearing the tables, putting paper plates and plasticware into a garbage bag.

"You don't have to do that," Mary said.

"It's the least I can do after enjoying such great hospitality."

Wayne Oliver joined them, apparently not surprised to find Todd there. "I didn't think you'd leave without saying good-bye."

"Todd's been cleaning up," Mary said.

Wayne Oliver unknowingly repeated her words. "You don't have to do that."

"It's my pleasure. I don't know when I've had a better time, Judge Oliver, or a better supper, Mary."

"I'm glad you remembered the day," Wayne Oliver said. "Now that you're back in Alabama, don't be a stranger."

Todd glanced at Mary. "I won't." He turned to shake her father's hand. "You may get tired of seeing me this summer. Good-bye and thanks again."

The Olivers walked Todd to the front door and watched his sporty pickup truck pull away from the curb.

Wayne Oliver rubbed his chin. "I wonder what Todd Walker plans to do in Rockdale this summer. Come to think of it, he didn't say where he works."

"I don't know, either," Mary said.

Seeing Todd again reminded Mary of the way girls had always flocked around him. He'd had his pick of the prettiest and the most popular ones, and he would never be interested in anyone who looked like her.

However, Todd Walker was a mature man now, and Mary believed he had really changed. She had a strange feeling he actually wanted to see her again.

Is that possible?

Mary sighed. *More like wishful thinking*, she told herself. She wouldn't get her hopes up, only to have them dashed.

four

The Rockdale Civic Improvement Association held its organizational meeting on the first Tuesday in June, and Judge Wayne Oliver was chosen as its leader. On the steering committee were Mayor Margaret Hastings; bank president Newman Howell; hardware store owner Sam Roberts; and Dr. Miles Endicott.

News of its formation received mixed reviews from Rockdale's citizens, who promptly dubbed it "the CIA." Some, like restaurant owner Tom Statum and Police Chief Earl Hurley, thought it was a good thing, while Sally Proffitt saw it as the beginning of the end of their town.

"I never saw anything with 'improvement' in it that didn't wind up costing us money," she told Oaks condo manager Nelson Neal in the checkout aisle at the Sack-and-Save grocery.

"I agreed and all I said to her was, 'We don't need any more taxes,'" Nelson explained.

But Sally Proffitt undoubtedly called Jenny Suiter as soon as she got home to report, "Nelson Neal says they're going to try to raise our taxes," because the rumor had spread through Rockdale like wildfire.

Seeing something must be done to clarify their position, Margaret Hastings suggested putting an article in the newspaper.

"We should also hold a public meeting to make sure everyone understands what we're trying to do," Sam Roberts said.

"Let's do both," Wayne Oliver urged. "With an article in this week's newspaper, we should have a good turnout for a meeting next week."

"Our work is cut out for us," Margaret Hastings said.

"Judge, why don't you ask Mary to write the article?"

❧

In the nine years Mary had been teaching, she'd never had an entire, uninterrupted summer vacation. The old saying that June, July, and August were the three best reasons for being a teacher had never applied to her. Between going to school several summers to earn her master's degree, traveling to conferences, and working on projects like the tenth reunion of her Rockdale High School graduating class, Mary had filled each summer.

"This year I'm going to work in the garden and catch up on my reading and that's it," Mary told anyone who asked about her summer plans. However, even before her father asked her to help the Civic Improvement Association, Mary realized she'd probably get little reading or gardening done this summer, either.

Her calendar was already full. Anita Sanchez's bridal tea was coming up on Sunday, and Mary was to serve at the reception following Anita's wedding to Hawk Henson the next Saturday. Vacation Bible School would be followed by school workshops and Toni's baby shower.

"No rest for the weary," Mary muttered as she began writing the Rockdale Civic Improvement Association article. When the telephone rang, she let the answering machine take the call. Hearing Walter's voice, Mary was glad she had.

"Hi, Mary. I know you must think I forgot all about you, but I'm back in town now. Call me, all right?"

Mary sighed and returned to work. Until she turned in the article, Walter would have to wait.

❧

Later that morning, Mary called Margaret Hastings and read her the completed article. "Will it do?"

"Yes, thank you. It's great. If you can take it in right away, Grant can put it in this week's *Record*."

Mary did as Margaret suggested, and Grant Westleigh, the publisher of the weekly newspaper, promised to feature the article on the front page of the next edition.

"I hope the Civic Improvement Association will be successful. The more folks who get involved, the better it'll be for Rockdale," he said. "I'm glad to do my part."

Relieved that chore was done, Mary left the newspaper office and headed for Statum's Family Restaurant, where she and her father planned to meet for lunch. She'd walked only a short distance when Walter Chance came out of his realty office and fell into step beside her.

"Hi, Mary. I saw you leaving the *Record*. I called earlier and got your answering machine."

"I just left an article about the Civic Improvement Association with Grant."

"They picked the right person to do it. You sure did a good job organizing our class reunion."

"That's ancient history."

"Two years isn't all that long. Anyway, I called to tell you your birthday gift will be here in a few days."

"I told you I didn't want anything."

"Too bad," Walter said cheerfully. "You're getting it anyway."

When Mary walked past her car without stopping, Walter spoke again. "Where are you going?"

"To Statum's for lunch."

Walter brightened. "Good—we can eat together."

"I'm meeting my father." Seeing Walter's face fall, she added, "I'm sure he won't mind if you join us."

When they reached the restaurant, Wayne Oliver immediately invited Walter to sit beside him. "I'm glad to see you. I need to talk to you about the Rockdale Civic Improvement Association."

He did so at some length, then listened as Walter offered a few suggestions. However, from the way he kept glancing at her, Mary got the impression Walter would rather have her to himself. When Judge Oliver left to return to the courthouse, Walter seemed genuinely sorry he had an appointment to list a property.

"I'll call you when your gift comes in. I can't wait for you to see it."

"Comes in? What is it?" Even though Mary didn't want anything from Walter, she was curious.

He grinned. "You'll find out."

≈

"Walter Chance has a good head on his shoulders," Mary's father said that evening. "Now that his mother's out of the picture, he seems to be using it. He knows the local real estate market, and I can tell he'll be a big help to the Rockdale Civic Improvement Association."

That's probably what my father had in mind when he invited Walter to the dinner.

"He seemed interested about it at lunch."

Her father looked amused. "When he wasn't making eyes at you, that is. I'd say Walter Chance seems to be smitten with you."

Mary shook her head. "You have it wrong. He's been lonely since his mother left town. He thinks of me as a good friend— that's all."

Wayne Oliver shook his head. "We'll see about that."

Mary glanced at her wristwatch and stood. "I have to make some Vacation Bible School calls, then I'm going to read awhile. I'll see you at breakfast."

In her room, Mary opened her Vacation Bible School note-book to the list of workers, but she found it hard to concentrate for thinking about her father's remarks.

I don't care what anyone says, Walter Chance is a friend, and that's all, she told herself.

Mary shook her head and sighed. God's call to teach His children was never far from her mind, and now she resolved to focus on the task at hand.

Lord, I put myself and all the Vacation Bible School workers in Your hands. Bless us and use us, according to Thy will.

Then she made her first call.

five

Mary had lost count of the number of bridal showers she had been involved with in the last ten years or so, but Anita Sanchez's was the fourth since the first of May. Mary had met Anita in January, when her daughter Juanita enrolled in Rockdale Elementary and was put in Mary's class. From the first, Mary had found Juanita to be a delightful little girl. When she made her usual visit to their home, Anita Sanchez had impressed Mary, as well. A widow living in public housing without much income, Anita had a quiet dignity that she managed to sustain even when a man who had followed her to Alabama from Texas kidnapped Juanita. The whole incident had lasted only a few hours, and the little girl had taken it in stride because, as she told her classmates, "God took real good care of me." Shortly afterward, when Juanita told Mary her mother and Rock County Deputy Hawk Henson were getting married, they had rejoiced together.

Mary knew Hawk had encountered a certain amount of prejudice because of his Cherokee heritage, and she suspected he'd felt a bond with Anita Sanchez, the first Hispanic to settle in Rockdale, who also knew what it was like to be "different."

All that was behind them now, and entering Community Church's fellowship hall on the second Sunday afternoon in June, Mary was glad to see the petite bride-elect. Anita was the lovely center of attention in a yellow dress, which set off her dark hair and eyes.

Toni Trent, one of the hostesses, pointed out the serving table. "Juanita and Mandy are helping—I heard Juanita ask if Miss Mary would be here."

Mary glanced at the long, lace-covered serving table where Juanita handed out napkins and Mandy poured punch. Both

33

girls were smiling and obviously enjoying themselves.

"Can I bring you some refreshment?" Toni asked Anita.

"No, thank you. I am too excited about seeing so many people today. I cannot eat or drink a thing."

Mary nodded in greeting to Margaret Hastings and Janet Brown, the wife of Community Church's music leader, then she and Toni walked toward the serving table. "Anita looks very happy," Mary commented.

"Believe me, after the hard time she's had the last few years, she deserves to be. She and Hawk both believe God meant for them to be together, and that's a wonderful foundation for their married life."

"Being in God's will is the best foundation for anyone's life," Mary said.

Toni glanced at her friend. "I know from experience God sometimes changes our perception of His will. I hope you're ready to accept it, should that happen to you. I think Walter Chance would like to be more than just a friend."

Mary ignored the comment and moved on ahead to greet Juanita and Mandy.

"This is a fun party, Miss Toni," Juanita said. "Miss Janet says they do this every time someone gets married."

"Just about," Toni agreed.

"Miss Janet told another lady Aunt Evelyn might need a tea soon," Mandy said.

Juanita looked puzzled. "But she's *old*."

Toni and Mary struggled not to smile. "Mandy's aunt isn't too old to be a bride," Toni said. "There isn't any age limit for that."

"Then when can I be a bride and have a party like this?" asked Juanita.

"When you're grown up and out of school," said Mandy, who enjoyed playing the role of big sister to Juanita.

"Let's get a glass of punch and sit down," Mary suggested to Toni. "You don't need to be on your feet all afternoon."

"You're as bad as David," Toni said. "He nags me all the time to take it easy."

They took their cups to a round table at the far end of the fellowship hall.

"Apparently the town has already decided Evelyn and your father will marry," Toni said.

"As I recall, the same thing happened with you and David. In your case, they were right."

Toni smiled. "So they were. Evelyn and Wayne obviously enjoy each other's company. I hope they'll be allowed to do so in peace."

"Changing the subject," Mary said, "my student teacher mentioned her cousin was Community's new associate pastor. I don't suppose he's here this afternoon."

Toni looked amused. "Jason Abbott? He hasn't officially started working, but even if he had, he'd hardly be at a bridal shower. And changing it back, you might as well get used to your father being part of a couple."

~

Mary returned home after the tea to find an empty house and a brief note from her father: "I won't be home for supper. Don't wait up."

On an impulse, she called Evelyn Trent's telephone number. She was not surprised when Evelyn's answering machine took the call.

Mary smiled wryly. It seemed their roles had suddenly been reversed. Now it was the father who went out on a date, while his daughter was advised not to wait up.

She had just hung up when the telephone rang. *Walter,* Mary guessed correctly.

"I'm glad I caught you at home. I have your gift, and I'd like to bring it over tonight, if that's all right."

Mary glanced at the clock. "I'm afraid not. I just got in, and I have a lot work to do."

"How about tomorrow night?"

"All right—seven o'clock."

"Great! See you then."

Mary replaced the receiver and wished she felt as enthusiastic about seeing Walter as he sounded about seeing her. She'd always liked Walter, perhaps in part because he'd had such a hard time—first dealing with the death of his father and then with a mother who'd tried to smother him. Mary considered him a good friend, and she knew friendship was the basis for many successful marriages. She also believed Walter Chance would make an excellent father. For the time being, however, Mary didn't see him as her potential husband.

Mary spread the Vacation Bible School material on the dining room table and began to work, determined to be ready for the first meeting with her committee.

❧

Mary's father hadn't come home by the time Mary retired for the night, but following his admonition, she didn't wait up for him. Just before she fell asleep Mary thought she heard his footsteps on the stairs, but she didn't get up.

By the time she came downstairs the next morning, her father had already left. "Early pretrial conference this morning and Bar Association dinner tonight," his note told her. "Home about nine."

By then, Mary hoped, Walter would already be gone.

❧

Mary reached First Church early, parked at the side of the building, and walked around to the front entrance. During the week when the sanctuary wasn't being used, it was closed off from the rest of the building to conserve energy, but it remained open for prayer.

Before the meeting, Mary went directly into the sanctuary. Having recently been at Community Church, Mary was struck by the contrast. She enjoyed attending special parties and programs at Community Church, and sometimes she went to a worship service when Toni Trent would be singing a solo. She rather admired Community's easy, informal style of worship, but for as long as Mary could remember, the more traditional First Church in downtown Rockdale had been an important part of her life.

From its Gothic-style native sandstone exterior to the massive oak double doors leading into the vaulted sanctuary, the building spoke to her of God's glory. As a child, she had spent hours studying the stained glass windows on either side of the velvet-cushioned dark wood pews. Even if they hadn't been placed there by long-ago Austin and Oliver ancestors, the two windows bearing their names would still have been Mary's favorites.

The Austin window showed Jesus as an infant, flanked by Mary and Joseph, with several angels looking down from the top of the window. In the Oliver window, Jesus blessed several children crowded around him. When Mary was about four years old, someone remarked she could have been the model for the chubby-cheeked little girl in the Savior's arms. Since the window had been placed there nearly a century earlier, the likeness was dismissed as an interesting coincidence. However, as a child Mary had liked to imagine herself resting in Christ's arms. Even when she was a grown woman and no one noticed any resemblance between herself and the child in the stained glass window, Mary still felt a sense of peace and protection each time she saw it.

Passing by the Austin and Oliver stained glass windows, Mary spent some time at the altar in prayer, asking God to help her concentrate on making this year's unusual VBS program a success.

"The traditional Bible story and crafts, juice, and cookies worked for generations of children, but we need to do something to get attendance back up to where it ought to be. See what you can find," First's educational director had urged during the March planning meeting.

Thus challenged by Reuben Martz, Mary and the committee had decided to adopt an entirely new concept for Vacation Bible School. Most of Mary's key workers had enthusiastically agreed, but a few grumbled they saw no reason to change anything.

Just like the town itself. Part of Rockdale seems perfectly content with the status quo, while others clamor for progress at any price.

In the end, they had worked out a compromise: The basic VBS framework would remain the same, but the program itself would be more varied and give the children different things to do.

Mary rose from prayer and went into the educational wing, following the chattering female voices to the meeting room.

"Hello, Mary," Melanie Neal greeted. "We were beginning to wonder what happened to you."

"I was in the sanctuary." Mary looked around the room at the women. With the exception of herself and Melanie, a fourth grade teacher at Rockdale Elementary, all were busy stay-at-home moms, and she knew they appreciated brief, to-the-point meetings. "Everyone's here except Alice Taylor, and she and her family are out of town this week. Let's have prayer, then we'll get started."

&

"I like the setup for this year's Bible school. You've come up with some really good ideas," Melanie Neal told Mary after the meeting. "We've never tried a field trip before."

"It took some talking to persuade Reuben Martz it could be done within our budget, but it'll be something for the kids to look forward to on the last day."

"Ronnie can't wait for VBS. He started whining about being bored two days after school ended," Melanie said.

Veronica Smith joined them and voiced her agreement. "Cassie would say that, too, except she knows I can always find work for her when she complains of having nothing to do."

"Whatever happened to the days when kids could enjoy doing nothing?" Melanie asked rhetorically.

"Television and video games, for starters," said Mary.

"I've got to go now," Veronica said. "Mandy Trent's staying with the kids, and she has to be somewhere else by lunchtime."

"Me, too—I have several errands to run," Doris Atwood said.

"Ronnie's at day camp, so I'm free until three o'clock,"

Melanie said when the others were gone. "Want to go some-where for lunch?"

"Sure. What do you have in mind?"

"If you have the time, we can go to DeSoto State Park," Melanie suggested.

"Fine. My father won't be home for supper. With a good lunch, I can do with a sandwich this evening."

"Since going out for lunch was my idea, I'll drive," Melanie volunteered.

Mary put her VBS materials in her Toyota's trunk and climbed into Melanie's SUV. "If this vehicle was any bigger, I'd need a ladder to get in."

"I know, but its size comes in handy when Ron and I haul Ronnie's soccer team all over Rock County."

As Melanie talked about the Neals' plans to take their son's team to a regional soccer tournament in Georgia, Mary felt the same near-envy she had begun to experience when women her age talked about their families. Last year, when Toni Schmidt had married David Trent and become an instant mother to Josh and Mandy, Mary's happiness for her friend had been mixed with a sense of regret that Toni had some-thing Mary never expected to experience. Lately, Mary had found herself yearning to be part of that kind of family so often she had begun to believe it might be God's way to let her know she should have her own family.

With a smile, Mary recalled her student's simple logic. *First, I'll need a husman.*

six

"I haven't been here since the weather turned warm," Mary said when they entered the DeSoto State Park Lodge.

"Ron likes the Sunday buffet, but so does everyone else. I'd rather come during the week when it's not so crowded."

"It certainly isn't crowded now," Mary observed. Just before the noon hour, only a few tables were occupied.

"Let's sit by the window," Melanie said. "I love to feel I'm in the middle of all these wonderful old trees."

After going through the buffet line, Mary and Melanie took their plates to a table overlooking the path to Lodge Falls and watched the dining room slowly fill with the usual mixture of casually dressed tourists and local men and women who worked in Ft. Payne, Rockdale, and other nearby towns. Mary had known quite a few of the diners all her life, but she didn't recognize the man who entered with the Community Church pastor.

"Who's that with Ed Hurley?" she asked Melanie.

"I don't know, but I suspect he might be Community Church's new assistant pastor. Ron's dad showed him an Oaks condo last week."

"My student teacher mentioned her cousin had been called to Community."

Almost as if Pastor Hurley had overheard their conversation, he brought his companion to their table. Although both men were casually dressed in short-sleeved sport shirts and summer slacks, the senior pastor bowed formally.

"Hello, ladies. Melanie Neal and Mary Oliver, may I present Community's new assistant pastor, Jason Abbott."

Of average height and size, with hazel eyes and wavy, light brown hair in need of cutting, Jason Abbott looked nothing like Mary expected. He wouldn't stand out in a crowd, yet something about him immediately appealed to Mary. His smile was infectious, and his grip was sure and firm when he shook her hand.

"Mary Oliver? My cousin Ann Ward told me to look you up. She said you were the best supervisor any student teacher could have," Jason said.

"Ann made my job easy—she's a natural teacher."

"I'm really glad to meet you, Mary," he said as if he meant it.

"It's a small world, isn't it?" Pastor Hurley asked rhetorically.

When Jason turned to shake Melanie's hand, Mary noted his shirt looked slept in and his slacks could use a good pressing. *Unlike his always-neat cousin, Jason Abbott must not care how he looks.*

Mary had scarcely made the judgment when a Bible verse came immediately to mind: *"The Lord does not look at the things man looks at. Man looks at the outward appearance, but the Lord looks at the heart."*

She had just met Jason Abbott, but Mary believed he must surely have a heart for the Lord—and that was what really mattered.

"Are you related to Nelson Neal?" Jason asked Melanie.

"He's my father-in-law. Will you be renting a condo at the Oaks?"

"Possibly."

"Mary also works with children at First Church," Ed Hurley said.

Jason Abbott regarded Mary with interest. "Really? Ann didn't tell me that. I'd like to talk with you about your Vacation Bible School. I understand First is trying something different this year."

"I'm not on the staff," Mary said quickly. "Reuben Martz is our educational director. He's in charge of VBS."

"Mary isn't a paid worker, but this is the third year Reuben has turned VBS over to her, and she also directs the children's Sunday school classes. She probably knows more about those programs than Mr. Martz," Melanie said.

Jason Abbott smiled. "You sound like Mary's agent."

"I just want to give credit where it's due," Melanie said.

"If you have time, I hope we can get together soon," Jason told Mary.

"Of course, for what it's worth."

Jason took a pen and small green notebook from his shirt pocket and wrote Mary's telephone number as she gave it. When he left their table, Jason nodded and smiled fleetingly. "Nice to meet you, ladies." To Mary, he added, "I'll call you."

When the men were safely out of earshot, Melanie turned to Mary. "What did you think of Jason Abbott?"

"He seems nice enough," Mary said cautiously. "My father would say he needs a haircut."

Melanie smiled. "I noticed that, too. He's not bad-looking, though, in a friendly puppy-dog sort of way."

"In any case, Community will probably like him."

❧

Mary returned home after lunch with Melanie to find three messages on the answering machine.

In the first, Walter Chance repeated he would be there at seven that night and added he couldn't wait for her to see his gift.

The second, from her father, reminded Mary he wouldn't be home for supper.

The third was a pleasant surprise.

"Hello, Mary and Judge Oliver. This is Todd Walker. I apologize for the short notice, but I'll be in Rockdale tomorrow and I'd like to take you both to lunch. I'll drop by the house about eleven. See you then."

Hearing Todd's mellow voice, Mary thought he could have been a radio announcer. Although he'd said he would be back to Rockdale often, Mary had doubted it. She listened to the message again, then left it on the machine for her father.

Todd will be here tomorrow. But tonight Mary was seeing Walter Chance.

æ

As Mary expected, Walter arrived promptly at seven. He had been the only Rockdale High reunion committee member who was always punctual. "One of my worst faults," he had said cheerfully when Mary tried to compliment him.

On this night, Walter had apparently taken even greater care with his appearance than usual. His hair was carefully combed, and his cotton sport shirt appeared to be new. The crease in his trousers was razor-sharp, and his shoes were freshly shined.

Unaccountably, Walter's neatness made her think of Jason Abbott's untidiness.

"You look very nice tonight," Mary said.

"You always do," Walter returned.

Mary's loose-fitting denim jumper had looked fine for the VBS meeting and lunch at DeSoto, but it was undeniably wrinkled, and she was embarrassed not to look her best, when Walter had taken such obvious pains with his appearance.

"Come in," she said belatedly.

Walter entered the hall and looked around. "Is the judge here?"

"No—he had a dinner obligation."

The news seemed to please Walter. "Here—happy birthday. I'm sorry it took me so long to get this to you."

Mary set the lavishly gift-wrapped package on the hall table. "This looks too pretty to open right away. Can I offer you a brownie and some lemonade?"

"Statum's supper special tonight included pecan pie, so I'll skip the brownie. I'll take a glass of your fine Oliver lemonade, though."

"I'll get it."

Walter followed Mary to the kitchen. "How many hours do you reckon we spent working on the reunion at this table?"

"A lot. Looking up addresses, making flyers—it all took time."

"I enjoyed every minute, though."

When they finished their lemonade, Mary rose from the

table. "We're not working tonight—we can sit in the living room."

"This is a wonderful house," Walter said. "It'd be perfect for a family with a bunch of children."

"It's not for sale," Mary said quickly.

"That's not what I meant." In the hall, Walter pointed to the package on the table. "Aren't you going to open it?"

"Of course. Let's sit down first." Mary took the gift into the living room, and Walter joined her on the sofa.

"I hope you like it. When I described you to the lady in the store, she said this should be just right."

It's probably just as well I didn't hear that conversation. Seeing the embossed gold seal of a prestigious Birmingham jewelry store on the package, Mary suspected Walter had spent more than he should have on her gift. When she removed the silver wrappings and looked at the contents of the rectangular, blue velvet-covered box inside, she was certain of it.

From a fine gold chain, a gemstone glowed with deep green fire. Mary had never seen anything like it, and she hardly knew what to say.

"Oh, Walter—this is far too fine."

"Not at all. I picked out the stone, and they set it just for you—that's what took so long. Here, I'll help you put it on."

Walter's fingers touched the nape of her neck when he fastened the clasp, and Mary shivered at the unexpected sensation.

Embarrassed, she went into the hall and stood before the mirror. The square-cut emerald brought out the green in her eyes and even added a touch of elegance to her denim jumper.

"It is a lovely necklace," she said, meaning it.

Walter smiled with pleasure. "It looks great on you, too. The stone is genuine—it came with papers."

"I've never had any jewelry with my birthstone," Mary said.

"Then it's time you did. I thought of your eyes the minute I saw this—I knew it would match them."

"I can't accept a gift like this," Mary began. She almost

finished the sentence with "from someone I'm not engaged to marry," but stopped short.

Walter stood behind Mary with his hands on top of her shoulders, then bent to kiss the nape of her neck. Surprised, Mary shivered. Flustered, she turned from the mirror and into Walter's arms, where he held her close for what seemed a very long time.

"I'm not very good at this, but you must know I think a lot of you," he murmured. "The store is holding the matching earrings for you."

Mary felt almost comfortable in Walter's embrace, but his last words brought her back to reality, and she backed away from him. "You shouldn't have done that."

Walter touched the silver hoop in one of Mary's earlobes. "I want you to have the earrings, too, but I didn't know if you had pierced ears."

"Yes, since seventh grade, but—"

"The earrings dangle." Walter pointed to an antique lamp in the living room. "Sort of like the things hanging on that shade."

"They're called prisms. The earrings sound lovely, but I can't accept them, either."

Walter shook his head and sighed. "You sound just like you did when we worked on the reunion, expecting everyone to do things your way."

His accusation took Mary aback. "You're saying I'm bossy?"

"No offense intended—that comes from being a teacher, since kids need a firm hand."

"Yes, they do."

Walter stepped closer and spoke with quiet urgency. "Maybe you haven't given it much thought, since you stay so busy, but don't you ever think about wanting to have kids of your own?"

His unexpected question startled Mary into a quick response. "You're right—I haven't given it much thought." *And I don't intend to discuss it with you tonight, either.*

Walter lifted his arms in mock surrender. "I'm sorry if that was out of line. Maybe I should leave before you throw me out."

Although he smiled, Mary sensed she'd hurt his feelings. "I would never do that. I do appreciate your gift."

"You really like it?"

"Of course—but you should return it to the store. I don't deserve it."

"Let me be the judge of that."

At the front door, Walter turned to give Mary a brief peck on her cheek. "The necklace will stay right here. You can wear it when we go out to celebrate your birthday."

"No. Anyway, one birthday party a year is more than enough, and I've already had two."

"I won't call it a birthday dinner, then. Being with you makes any day a special occasion."

Mary heard his flowery words in disbelief. If Walter Chance ever had any romantic interest in her, he'd kept it well hidden, and she hardly knew what to make of the sudden change in him. "We had some good times working together, but—"

"We'll have even better ones in the years to come, I hope." Walter pulled Mary close and kissed her as if he really thought of her as more than his good friend. "I really do enjoy being with you," he said when he finally let her go.

Mary realized Walter probably expected her to offer a similar sentiment, but she could not. His kiss—and her reaction to it—had temporarily rendered her incapable of saying what she should. "Good night, Walter."

He smiled. "Take care, now."

Mary leaned against the door, relieved he was gone, at least for the time being.

His gift was by far the most valuable she'd received from any man other than her father. Even in the relatively dim hall, the emerald captured and reflected bursts of light.

Wondering if she looked as strange as she felt, Mary

returned to look into the hall mirror. Color infused her cheeks, and her eyes glowed with the same hue as the emerald. The necklace became her, all right, but she should have refused it immediately.

Should she accept and wear Walter's gift, Mary felt it would send him—and everyone who saw it—a mistaken message.

Mary removed the necklace and replaced it in its velvet nest. She would show it to her father when he came home, but as lovely as it was, she couldn't keep it.

She would return Walter's gift with gratitude—and the heartfelt hope Walter Chance would understand.

seven

"I take it you got my messages about the Bar Association meeting," Wayne Oliver said when he came home that evening.

"Yes. However, I didn't know you were going out last night."

"I'd like to talk to you about that."

"I have something to discuss with you, too."

He smiled faintly. "Let's adjourn to the study, then."

Mary had always liked the mahogany-paneled room with its floor-to-ceiling array of books. When she was very small, she had longed for the day when she would be able to take a book from any shelf and read every word of it. By the time she was old enough to do so, Mary was disappointed to find most of the tomes had to do with the law—Wayne Oliver's father before him had also been a lawyer—and, in her opinion, the books made very dull reading. However, the room was furnished with a couch and several comfortable chairs. As a child, Mary had often done her schoolwork at a table beside the window while her father worked on the mysterious papers in his briefcase—"my homework," as he called it.

Her father moved one of the overstuffed chairs to face the other, as he had done through the years when he wanted to have a heart-to-heart talk with Mary. She always supposed it was so he could see her face and gauge her reaction to his words.

Wayne Oliver leaned back in his chair and steepled his fingers, much as he did when he was about to hear a case in his court. "I'm sorry if I caused you concern last night, but at the last minute Evelyn decided she wanted to go to an arts festival in Huntsville. After we took it in, we stopped for dinner on the way home. We were gone a few hours longer than I expected. I suppose I should have called, but time got away from me."

"I wasn't worried—and I'm glad you and Evelyn are going out. You probably know it's causing some talk around town, though."

He nodded. "Unfortunately, some people have nothing better to do than talk about their neighbors. We knew gossip could be a problem, but Evelyn and I don't let it bother us."

"It doesn't bother me, either—and I wish you both well."

Her father leaned forward and touched Mary's cheek tenderly. "I'm glad you feel that way. I didn't think you'd mind, but this a new situation for me."

Mary smiled. "Rockdale may be in for a lot of new things."

Her father settled back into his chair. "So it seems. Now it's your turn—what's on your mind?"

"I want to show you something."

"That's a mighty fancy box," her father commented when Mary returned with it.

"Walter brought it over this evening as a birthday gift."

"That was thoughtful."

"I'm not sure 'thoughtful' is the right word. Open it."

Wayne Oliver's startled expression confirmed Mary's belief the emerald pendant was no ordinary bauble. "The stone looks like the real thing. I'm surprised Walter Chance can afford a piece like this."

"Even worse, he wants to give me the matching earrings."

Her father shook his head. "I knew Walter cared for you, but this is more than an ordinary gift."

"I know—I tried to tell him he shouldn't have given it to me, but he wouldn't listen."

"You like Walter, don't you? You seem to get along well."

"Of course, but suddenly he seems to think we're much more than friends. Grandmother Oliver would say a girl shouldn't accept any expensive gift unless she and the man are engaged, and I've decided not to keep it."

Her father returned the box to Mary. "I hardly know what to say. Rules about accepting gifts have changed since my mother's day. Walter will probably feel hurt if you return it, but if it makes you uncomfortable, you shouldn't keep it."

"That's what I thought. I'll give it back tomorrow."

Wayne Oliver stood and winced as he rubbed the shoulder he'd injured playing football years before. "Is that all we have to discuss?"

"Yes," Mary said, then belatedly remembered. "One more thing—Todd Walker left us a message on the machine."

Her father looked puzzled after hearing it. "I wonder what brings Todd to Rockdale in the middle of the week?"

"I suppose we'll find out tomorrow."

"You'll have to do that on your own. With a full court docket, I won't have time to go out for lunch."

"Todd didn't leave a number where he could be reached," Mary said. "It would serve him right if he found nobody at home."

Her father smiled. "I doubt you'll allow that to happen. Maybe Todd will take you somewhere nice."

"Melanie Neal and I had lunch at DeSoto today, but Todd may already have something in mind."

"I suspect he does," her father said dryly.

&

Tuesday morning found Mary with mixed feelings about the day ahead. While she looked forward to seeing Todd Walker, she dreaded the necessary encounter with Walter Chance.

During her morning quiet time, Mary prayed more earnestly than usual for God's guidance. She had always trusted His leadership, but lately Mary had felt confused about the source of her changing feelings about marriage.

Never accept your own wishful thinking as the Lord's will. 'Thy will be done' must be part of every petition. Mary didn't remember where or when she'd heard the admonition, but it often came to her mind when she prayed for guidance.

Show me Your will for my life, Lord.

Mary didn't expect God to speak to her directly in a voice from above, but she trusted He knew what was best for her and would make it clear to her in due time.

For now, she still felt she had to return the emerald pendant. Even if Walter Chance should turn out to be the man God meant for her, Mary couldn't accept his gift now.

At nine o'clock Mary called Walter's office and felt relieved to hear he had gone to a property closing. Since he wasn't there, she could return the necklace without seeing him—at least immediately.

Mary composed a quick note telling Walter she appreciated his thoughtfulness and valued his friendship, but she couldn't accept such a valuable gift. Signing it "Your friend always," Mary then printed Walter's name on a manila envelope, put the note and the jeweler's box inside, and sealed it with mailing tape.

Ten minutes later she handed the package to Ellie Fergus, Chance Realty's forty-something receptionist, and asked her to give it to Walter.

"He'll probably be tied up until lunchtime. Do you want him to call you when he returns?"

"No—that's not necessary."

Mary knew Walter would probably try to contact her as soon as he opened the package, but by then she'd be with Todd Walker. For the moment, Todd was all that mattered.

❧

Mary surveyed the contents of her closet and debated what she should wear. Todd had already seen her in her worst baggy jeans and oversized shirt, so almost anything else would be an improvement. She wanted to look presentable without going overboard to impress him.

After several false starts, Mary finally chose a two-piece red linen dress she'd had for several years. With the proper accessories, it was the kind of outfit that could be worn anywhere, at any time. She almost hadn't bought it, thinking the color called attention to her size. Instead, the salesclerk had assured her it suited her coloring perfectly. "Red is a powerful color for women who can wear it, and you definitely can."

Today Mary chose simple silver hoop earrings and a slender silver necklace to complete the image of an independent young woman who wasn't afraid to dress boldly.

I don't know why I'm going to all this trouble. Todd Walker was out of my league when I was a teenager, and I'm past the point of playing dating games now.

When the telephone rang shortly after ten-thirty, Mary's first thought was Walter had come back to the office early, or that Todd wouldn't be there after all, leaving her all dressed up with no place to go. However, Mary relaxed when she heard a familiar feminine voice at the other end of the line.

"Mary, this is Janet Brown."

In addition to playing for Community Church's worship services, Janet gave private piano lessons to many of Mary's former first-graders and helped with Rockdale Elementary's annual musical program. Mary steeled herself, fearful Janet was about to ask her help with something.

"Hi, Janet. What's up?"

"I'm calling to invite you and Judge Oliver to a reception in the Community Church fellowship hall Sunday afternoon to welcome Jason Abbott, our new associate pastor."

Mary decided not to tell Janet she'd already met him, since it had no bearing on whether she and her father attended the reception. "What time?"

"From two until four. I especially want Pastor Abbott to meet you and the judge. We think he's a great addition to Rockdale."

"Thanks, Janet. We'll try to be there."

Pastor Abbott. It was the first time Mary had heard Jason called by his formal title. *He probably looks more dignified when he's in church.*

Mary wrote "Community, 2–4:00" in next Sunday's square on the calendar beside the kitchen telephone, then she surveyed the current week.

For Tuesday, Mary's father had written "RCIA Mtg 7:00." The Rockdale Civic Improvement Association would hold an open forum in the high school auditorium the next week, and Mary figured she'd be expected to attend the Tuesday night meeting and make notes for another article.

On Wednesday the Olivers usually attended the fellowship supper and midweek services at First Church. Mary had marked Friday night for the rehearsal dinner for Anita and Hawk's wedding and Saturday for the wedding and reception, at which she was serving.

Now, with the addition of Sunday's reception for Jason Abbott, Mary had managed to fill nearly every day with some sort of activity.

So much for a leisurely vacation.

Just as Mary capped her pen, the doorbell rang. On her way to answer it, her glance at the grandfather clock confirmed that Todd Walker was ten minutes early. No time to double-check her hair and makeup—but Mary supposed she probably looked as good as she ever would.

Todd had his hand extended, ready to ring the doorbell again, when she opened the door.

"There you are," he said. "I was beginning to think no one was home."

"Come in," Mary invited.

"Wow," Todd said when she turned to face him. His admiration seemed genuine, and Mary didn't know to react.

"You look better, too." As soon as she said it, Mary wished she could take back the comment. However, it was true: From his dress shirt, worn without a tie and open at the neck, to his dark slacks and shined tassel loafers, Todd Walker looked every inch like a very handsome junior executive.

"Thanks. I've been told I clean up pretty well. Is the judge here?"

"No. He sends his regrets, but he doesn't have time to go out for lunch today."

Perhaps it was Mary's imagination, but she thought Todd

looked pleased her father wasn't joining them.

"I was afraid of that, but I'm glad to see you."

"You almost didn't. This is a busy week, and I might not have been here. You should have left your number."

Todd shrugged. "It wouldn't matter. I had to be in the vicinity today, and I hoped lunch would work for us—and apparently it has."

Mary acknowledged the failure of her mild reprimand and returned his smile. "I'll get my purse, then we can go."

eight

"I don't usually have lunch this early," Mary told Todd as they made their way down the boxwood-bordered brick walk to the street.

"Neither do I, but it won't be so early by the time we get where we're going."

At the end of the walk, Mary stopped and stared at the vehicle at the curb, a fire-engine red convertible with the top down. "What happened to your truck?" she asked.

"Nothing, but this is a lot more fun to drive. Besides, it matches your dress." Todd opened the convertible's door for Mary. "I can put the top up if you like."

She shook her head. Although she didn't want to admit it to Todd, Mary had never ridden in a convertible, and she was curious to know what it was like. "Don't put it up on my account. My hair is so short, wind won't hurt it."

"You won't feel much wind in your hair in this car, but it's bright today—your eyes will need protection."

Her father had given Mary a stylish new pair of sunglasses for her birthday, and when she removed them from her purse and put them on, Todd whistled in appreciation.

"You look like a movie star, Miss Oliver. I can see myself reflected in your lenses, but I can't see your eyes."

Todd turned the key in the ignition and the car roared to life. To Mary, the motor had the rich sound of the stock cars she'd seen at a NASCAR race at Talladega. Directly across the street, Sally Proffitt must have had a similar thought, because she came out of her house and shaded her eyes as if looking to see what was making so much noise.

Mary groaned inwardly, aware that Sally Proffitt would probably waste no time calling Jenny Suiter. She had a good idea what Sally might say: *You won't believe this, but Mary Oliver just rode off in a fancy red convertible with a* man.

By suppertime, the news would be all over town.

Mary didn't think Todd had noticed Sally Proffitt's neck craning, but after making a U-turn in the street and heading back toward town, he laughed. "Maybe we ought to go back and give your neighbor an encore performance. It's obvious she enjoyed the first show."

"That's Sally Proffitt. She's a widow without much to do since her children grew up and moved away. She thinks it's her job to know everything going on around here."

"I know the type," Todd said. "She's probably also tried to persuade the judge he needs a wife."

Mary smiled at his accurate depiction. "I think she did at one point, but Rockdale's widows gave up on my father a long time ago. He calls Sally Proffitt and her best friend Rockdale's two-woman gossip tag team. What one doesn't know, the other finds out. Then they share the results of their investigations with everyone who'll listen."

"I hope riding in my car won't ruin your reputation," Todd said lightly.

"Even Sally Proffitt couldn't do that," Mary replied. For better or worse, no one in Rockdale was likely to believe Judge Oliver's schoolmarm daughter capable of doing anything wrong.

When Todd turned onto the main road leading out of town, she reminded him he hadn't said where they were going.

"Since we don't have to worry about getting Judge Oliver back to court on time, there's something I want to show you."

"A new restaurant?"

"Not exactly. You'll see. Lean back and enjoy the ride."

It was a perfect early June day, and Todd maneuvered the red car expertly around the twists and turns of the road out of Rockdale. Mary liked the new sensation of openness and freedom of riding in the convertible. She relished the feeling she was one with everything around her—the welcome breeze, the cloudless sky, even the flickering shadows of passing trees.

On the other hand, Mary knew her unshaded face would soon be as red as her dress. *So much for glamour—it never was my style, anyway.*

"We must be going to Mentone," Mary said when they reached the main highway and Todd turned in that direction.

"Close."

He passed Mentone and turned the car into a rutted lane a few miles on the other side. The going was so rough Mary grasped her armrest with both hands, convinced her safety belt was the only thing keeping her from being thrown out of the car altogether.

"Sorry," Todd muttered when they hit a particularly rough spot. "That was the worst part."

He continued driving until the road ended abruptly at a fencerow after a few hundred more yards. Several nearby trees had faded but still prominent signs that read: POSTED: NO HUNTING, NO FISHING, NO TRESPASSING. Behind them, dust stirred by the car's tires still hung in the air. Mary felt a thin film of grit when she ran her tongue over her dry lips—and imagined it had permeated every fiber of her suit, as well. *I got dressed up for this?*

"It's not as bad as it looks," Todd assured her. "This is as close as we can get to the gate—it's just up the way."

"The gate to what?"

"Something special. Watch your step, now—this is uneven ground."

You can say that again. Mary's open-toed sandals were no match for the loose dirt and sticks littering the ground. "I have to stop. I think there's a small boulder in my shoe," she said after walking a short distance.

There was no place to sit down, but Todd took Mary's left arm and held her steady while she balanced on one foot, crane-like, and removed debris from first one sandal, then the other. "You should have told me to change my shoes before we left the house," she said.

"I didn't think about it," Todd admitted. "Anyway, we're almost there."

Todd continued to hold Mary's arm, guiding her around a nest of fire ants and through a rusty gate. On the other side, a narrow, crooked path wandered toward a rock outcropping.

"That's a deer trail," Mary noted.

"I see you know your way around the woods."

Mary detected a note of respect in Todd's voice. "Yes, but I don't usually track deer while wearing open-toed sandals."

Todd chuckled. "I like your sense of humor. Most women take themselves far too seriously."

Maybe so, but full-figured women like me pretend to be jolly at all times—it's expected of us.

"So do some men," she said, and let it go at that.

If Todd heard her, he made no comment. They reached the rock outcropping, and Todd stepped up onto it and turned to help Mary. "Here we are."

If I fall now, I'll probably break something major and disgrace myself forever. Mary kept her eyes down and concentrated on keeping her footing. With a final effort, she found a secure foothold and pulled herself up to stand on the rock beside him.

"Well, what do you think?" Todd asked.

Mary looked up and gasped in admiration at the view before them. The rock on which they stood bordered a bluff overlooking a heavily wooded valley. To the right, a waterfall bisected an adjacent ridge. Its sparkling waters spilled over the top of the mountain, then cascaded into a meandering stream in the valley below. "It's beautiful," she said. "Where are we?"

"In one of those well-kept secret places locals keep to themselves."

"How do you know about it?" asked Mary.

Todd smiled. "I'll tell you about it over lunch, but I wanted you to experience it first."

"Thank you. A view like this is definitely worth a few rocks in my shoes."

"I'm glad you agree."

Todd smiled, apparently pleased with her reaction. He took Mary's hand to help her down, then continued to hold it on the walk back to the car. "Now we'll have lunch," he said.

Todd drove back to Mentone and stopped at a restaurant located in an old Victorian house near the bluff. Mary had been there several times, and she knew the rear windows offered a pleasant view of the valley below. However, the panorama they had just seen was much more spectacular.

The dining room was nearly filled, but the hostess led them to a just-vacated table in the rear.

Mary excused herself as soon as the waitress had taken their orders. "I'll be eating dirt and drinking mud if I don't wash the dust from my face first," she told Todd.

"I don't remember the lane being that dusty—I suppose it's because it hasn't rained here lately."

In the dim light of the mirror in the ladies' room, Mary dabbed a wet paper towel to her mouth and forehead and noted the sun had already affected her skin. *I'll probably be burned to a crisp by the time I get back home.*

Mary sighed. In her childhood, her fair complexion had freckled when she stayed out in the sun too long, but in recent years, her unprotected skin merely went from pink to red. She always used a high-numbered sunblock and wore a hat when she gardened or was outdoors for a long time. However, today she hadn't thought to do either. She'd enjoyed riding in Todd's convertible, but the resulting sunburn would be a different matter.

Todd stood when Mary returned to the table. "Feel better?" he asked.

"Much."

He looked at her closely. "The color in your cheeks is quite becoming, but I'm afraid you've gotten too much sun."

Mary felt she would be blushing if her face weren't already

red. "I'm told I inherited my mother's fair skin. I should have worn my floppy-brimmed red hat."

Todd smiled. "You had on a country-gal straw hat at the cemetery. I can imagine you in a floppy-brimmed hat—Mary Oliver, Southern belle, holding an armful of—of petunias or whatever pretty flowers you grow in that garden of yours."

Mary smiled at his fanciful description. She had never thought of herself as a Southern belle, and she was sure no one else had, either. "I don't think you'd see me with an armful of petunias. Most of the flowers in our garden are perennials—since they come back every year, they require very little work. We usually plant several flats of annuals for color, but I rarely have armfuls of anything."

"Maybe you'll give me an educational tour of your garden. I admit to being an ignoramus when it comes to flowers."

"Most men are," Mary said. She was about to tell him her father had proved to be an exception when the waitress brought their food.

After a while, Todd looked out of the window and pointed to the patchwork of fields and woods in the valley below. "You know, this entire area is really one of the best-kept secrets in the country. I had almost forgotten how green Alabama is."

"I suppose it is, compared to much of the West."

"Some of California is naturally green, but I spent most of my time in the desert. There wasn't enough available water for nonessential irrigation, so most landscaping consisted of rocks and sand and cactus plants."

"That sounds grim."

"I thought so, too. I never really got used to it. Even the weeds around here look beautiful to me, so long as they're green."

"You were going to tell me about the place we just saw," Mary prompted.

Todd watched Mary dip her fork into the container of raspberry vinaigrette dressing beside her plate and then into her garden salad. "That's a good idea," he said. "Too much dressing spoils a salad's taste."

And cuts down the calories. Although true, it was not something Mary wanted to share with Todd Walker. "True. Now what about that bluff property?"

Todd poured ketchup on his plate and dipped a few French fries in it before he spoke.

"It's ten acres in all, too rocky to farm and too poor to support any livestock except goats. It's been in the Millican family for years, although none of them lives here now. Herman Millican tried to sell it about ten years ago, but nobody wanted to buy it then. His son inherited it, and when I finally tracked him down in Key West, he said he might consider selling for the right price."

"I don't suppose he's put it on the market?"

"No. It would have been snapped up by the first person who saw it."

"Assuming you're that person, are you going to buy it?"

Todd speared a French fry and pushed it around his plate, then looked back at Mary. "I'd like to buy it for myself, but actually I scouted it for my company."

His company? "I don't think you ever said where you work."

"Haskell Holdings—you probably never heard of it."

"You're right, but I don't know much about the business world."

Todd warmed to his subject. "Haskell Holdings is a large conglomerate composed of many separate companies, ranging from small to large. Among other things, it provides venture capital."

"Exactly what do you do for this conglomerate?"

"Lots of things. For one, I find opportunities for investment for the Holdings' companies."

"Like the Millican land?"

Todd smiled his approval. "You got it. I'm also going to be doing some scouting around Rockdale."

"For land?"

"Not necessarily."

Todd leaned toward Mary and seemed about to say more, but just then an attractive young woman with honey-blond hair appeared at their table. When she spoke Todd's name, he rose to greet her.

Mary inspected the newcomer. Almost Todd's height and reed-slender in white slacks and a designer top, she had the kind of tan probably acquired from lazing on white sand beaches. Her perfectly manicured nails made Mary want to hide her imperfect gardener's hands. From head to toe, the young woman oozed charm and self-assurance.

"I didn't expect to see you here today," she said.

Todd seemed slightly flustered. "Same here."

The blond looked at Mary. "I don't believe we've met."

"Sorry—I seem to have left my manners at home today," Todd said quickly. "Mary, meet Veronica Lindsay. Veronica works for Haskell Holdings, too."

Veronica took Mary's hand, but her expression suggested she thought Mary must have crawled out from under one of the local rocks. "Hello, Mary Oliver. And just what do *you* do?"

"Mary is a teacher," Todd put in quickly.

"How nice." Veronica's tone denied the words.

Mary's pasted-on smile flickered, then faded. She glanced at Todd, then looked back to Veronica. "He didn't mention my main claim to fame."

Todd and Veronica both seemed surprised. "Really? What is that?" Veronica asked.

"Todd Walker is my cousin."

nine

All her life, Mary had experienced bouts of what she called "foot-in-mouth disease." Especially under stress, Mary found herself saying things she instantly regretted and later agonized over. Her words occasionally hurt others, but for the most part, Mary bore the brunt of her own speech. She recognized herself in the third chapter of the book of James and often prayed for the strength to tame her tongue when it threatened to become "a flame of fire."

However, the looks on Todd's and Veronica's faces when she declared her kinship to Todd had been priceless. His mouth had dropped open, and Veronica seemed to be pleased.

"It was nice to meet you," she told Mary. "Sorry, but I have to run."

After Veronica drifted away, Todd sat back down and stared at Mary. "Why did you tell her that?"

"I don't know," Mary confessed. "At least it's the truth."

"It's more like a half truth. Anyway, I think you shocked Veronica."

Good. She looks like she needs some shaking up. But this time, Mary kept the thought to herself.

&

When they left the restaurant, Todd put up the convertible top. "You've had enough sun for one day," he told Mary.

"I don't tan well," she said. *Unlike Miss Veronica.*

Todd smiled. "You turn pink very nicely, though."

"Did you say you work with Veronica?" Mary asked as they started back to Rockdale.

"She's at Haskell Holdings, but we don't report to the same boss."

"It's odd you both wound up in Mentone the same day."

He shrugged. "Coincidences happen all the time." His tone suggested Todd didn't want to talk about Veronica, and she took the hint.

"How long after you left California did you start working in Birmingham?"

"It was quite awhile. When I quit my job out there and came back to Alabama, I didn't have anything else lined up."

"That took a lot of faith," Mary said.

"More like a lot of stupidity. I studied the 'Help Wanted' ads and sent out dozens of résumés without ever getting a nibble. I was nearly broke and ready to take almost any kind of work when I ran into a guy I'd played football with at Alabama."

"I suppose he worked for Haskell Holdings," Mary said.

"Yes—how did you know that?"

"It was just a guess." Too late, Mary realized she should have let Todd finish his own story.

"Anyway, Kurt Talbott hired on there several years ago. He got me an appointment with his boss, and a week later I became part of the HH family."

Since Veronica also works there, does that mean she can also claim to be your kin? Wisely, Mary suppressed the sharp words.

After Todd spent several more minutes enumerating the benefits of his Haskell Holdings employment, Mary told him it sounded like a good place to work.

"It is. And best of all, it let me have a chance to take my favorite cousin out to lunch."

Mary saw no need to reply, especially since they had reached Rockdale and were only blocks away from her house. However, when Todd stopped the car at the curb and came around to open her door, courtesy demanded her to invite him to stay longer.

"I'll give you that educational garden tour now if you have time," she said.

"Sorry, but I don't. I still have to check in at the office this afternoon. Maybe I can take you up on it some other time."

"I hope you will. Thanks for lunch—and for letting me see that bluff property. I hope your deal works out."

"So do I."

Todd walked Mary to her front door and waited while she unlocked it. "I can remember a time when no one in Rockdale locked their doors," Todd said.

"Unfortunately, that's no longer safe, even here."

"Still, the town seems pretty much the same as it's always been."

"For better or worse." Mary started to tell Todd about the Rockdale Civic Improvement Association, then decided against it. He should get back to Birmingham, and she needed to go inside and treat her sunburn.

"Better, I think." Todd gave Mary a cousinly peck on the cheek. "I hope to see you soon," he said, then turned and walked back to his car.

I hope to see you soon. Was it merely a polite good-bye to a relative, or did Todd mean it more personally?

Todd turned and waved when he reached his car. Mary waved back, then glanced across the street. Sally Proffitt was sitting in her porch swing, no doubt having watched every move she and Todd had made.

That woman needs a pair of binoculars. She's headed for a bad case of eyestrain.

❧

"What's that white goop on your face?" Mary's father asked at supper that evening.

"Ointment. We went to lunch in Todd's convertible, and I got sunburned."

"Todd Walker has a convertible? You should have worn a hat. Where did you go?"

"To the restaurant in Mentone you like."

"I'm sorry I couldn't join you, but it's just as well I didn't try. I had to declare a mistrial in the Gessman case, and two other cases I'd expected to plead decided to go forward to trial."

Mary knew her father enjoyed discussing his work, since

she kept what he said confidential.

"Did Todd say why he was in town today?" he asked when he finished recounting his day in court.

"Not exactly, but I think Haskell Holdings might be looking to buy property around Mentone." Mary decided against identifying the Millican land. It had nothing to do with Rockdale, and although Todd hadn't asked her to keep quiet, she gathered he didn't want others to know about the bluff land.

"So that's where Todd works."

"What do you know about it?"

"Not much. Haskell Holdings is a rather new megacompany with too many irons in the fire, in my opinion. Which division is he in?"

"I don't know, but apparently one of his Alabama football teammates who already worked there was responsible for his being hired."

Wayne Oliver chuckled. "Ah, the good old buddy system in action. There are some positive things to be said about collegiate sports, after all. I hope Todd comes our way again. I'd like to get to know him better."

So would I. Seeing Todd again had reminded Mary of the feelings she had once had for him. Those days of puppy love were gone, but her interest in Todd Walker was not.

"I hope you'll be here the next time he comes."

"What about Walter? I don't suppose you had time to see him today."

"No—I tried, but he wasn't in his office this morning."

"So you still have the necklace?"

Mary shook her head. "I asked Ellie Fergus to give it to him. So far, he hasn't called."

"I'm surprised," Wayne Oliver said.

So am I.

Her father looked at his watch. "I don't want to be late for the Civic Improvement Association meeting."

"I'd forgotten all about that."

"We need another article, and you did a good job on the

first one. You should come with me tonight."

Mary didn't really feel up to going out. Her arms weren't quite as sunburned as her face, but when she'd put on a sleeveless shift after showering, the line where her red linen suit sleeve had ended and her sunburn began was quite clear. Ordinarily, she would have begged off, but this evening was different.

"Where is it, and who will be there?"

"The Endicotts'. It'll be me, Margaret Hastings, Newman Howell, Sam Roberts, and Miles Endicott."

Walter Chance wouldn't be there. "All right, but I hope the air conditioning works—my face feels like it's on fire."

❧

Walter didn't call that night, nor did Mary hear from him the next morning. She alternated between being glad he hadn't called to wishing he would so she could know the matter of the necklace had been resolved once and for all.

Mary tried to concentrate on writing the second Rockdale Civic Improvement Association article, an open invitation to all Rockdale residents to come to the high school auditorium for an informational meeting the following Tuesday night. However, since the committee wanted to make sure the article would arouse enough interest to produce a good turnout, Mary took special pains with it.

When she handed the article to Grant Westleigh, he looked it over and nodded his approval. "Just a minute," he said when Mary turned to leave. "Don't you also have an item for the 'Around Rockdale' personals column?"

Mary knew Grant was teasing her. She had a pretty good idea why, but she decided to pretend otherwise. "Not unless my meeting of First Church Vacation Bible School's steering committee qualifies for the Personals."

"I had in mind something more like this: 'Miss Mary Oliver recently entertained Mr. First Name Unknown, Last Name Unknown, of Birmingham, who took her for a ride lasting several hours in his red convertible. Miss Oliver is recovering from her resulting sunburn at the Oliver ancestral home in Rockdale.'"

Mary laughed. "I believe I know the source of that piece of information, but I wonder how she knew the unnamed mister lives in Birmingham."

"Maybe it's because she can read a license tag from a distance of, say, across a street. How about filling in the blanks?"

Mary knew she could trust Grant Westleigh to keep a confidence. "There's nothing secret about it, but it's hardly front-page news. The car in question is Todd Walker's. You probably remember him—he was a Rockdale High football star who went on to play at Alabama."

"Sure, I do. Isn't he kin to you?"

Only a relative would be taking someone like Mary Oliver for a ride in a convertible. Grant Westleigh might not think so, but she knew many others probably would.

"Todd and I are distant cousins."

Grant Westleigh grinned. "Kissin' cousins, as we say in the South. Is he moving back here?"

"No. Todd works for Haskell Holdings."

"Which, of course, happens to be in Birmingham."

"At least Sally Proffitt got that part right," Mary said ruefully.

The newspaperman put his index finger to his lips. "Hush, now. You know I can't divulge my sources."

"I hope you won't repeat what I said to your 'sources,' either. Come to think of it, I suppose we should have told Sally Proffitt and Jenny Suiter there'd be a secret meeting of the Rockdale Civic Improvement Association. The word would be all over town a lot sooner than this article can be printed."

"At least in a garbled version. I've noticed that those ladies' stories always manage to get at least one detail wrong."

"Otherwise, they'd make a great addition to your staff. Good-bye, Grant. Thanks for your help."

"Glad to be of service. Take care of that sunburn."

Mary was still smiling as she left the *Record* office. Since Sally Proffitt had spread the news of what she'd seen all over town, she supposed it was better to laugh about it than to be bothered.

Mary was about to get into her car when Walter Chance came out of his office and almost literally blocked her way.

"Hello, Mary. Do you have a minute?"

ten

Here it comes—Walter has found the envelope. Mary glanced at her watch as if she had something pressing to do, but Walter ignored the gesture.

"I want to show you something. It'll take thirty minutes, tops."

Mary didn't know whether to be relieved or alarmed. *Surely he must have opened the envelope by now—or has he?* She decided not to bring it up first.

"I suppose I can spare that much time."

Walter finally noted her sunburn and did a double take. "Wow—how did you get that?"

"By not wearing a hat when I should have."

"You don't need any more sun."

Walter took Mary's arm and steered her toward his building. "My car's in the parking lot out back. I'll just stop and tell Ellie I'm leaving."

Ellie Fergus sat at her desk, talking on the telephone. She waved at Mary, then covered the phone's mouthpiece to speak to Walter. "This is a man who's staying at the Rockdale Inn and wants to see the Johnson house. When can you show it?"

Walter signaled for the telephone, and Ellie handed it to him. "Hello, this is Walter Chance. How can I help you?"

Mary leaned close to Ellie and spoke in a whisper. "Did you give Walter the envelope I left here yesterday?"

"I put it on his desk. Do you want me to see if it's still there?"

"No—it's not important."

Certain Walter hadn't opened the envelope, she didn't want him to do so yet.

Walter continued to speak with enthusiasm as he described

a property Mary knew well. The vacant farmhouse on the edge of town had looked extremely run-down last July when she and Toni drove by it on their way to take the Trent children to pick wild blackberries. Mary and Toni had reminisced about the time Toni lived there in foster care in her teens, before Judge Oliver gave Evelyn Trent custody of the girl so many others had called "terrible Toni Schmidt."

"It's sad the house wasn't kept up after the Johnsons left town," Toni remarked that day, and Mary had agreed.

Hearing Walter's glowing account of the place, Mary recalled her father's words: *Walter Chance has a good head on his shoulders.* He was certainly making a success of the family business, and Mary could see why he was regarded as a good catch.

"I can pick you up at one, if that's convenient. Good. See you then, Mr. Andrews."

Walter returned the telephone to Ellie, who noted the appointment on the office calendar. "I'll be out of the office for about thirty minutes. Don't call my cell phone unless it's a true emergency."

"Yes, Mr. Chance."

"Sorry for the interruption." Walter led Mary down the hallway, past a conference room, his office and those of the other two Chance Realty agents who worked there, and into the small parking lot.

Of the cars parked there, Walter's beige Towncar was the largest and most luxurious. Walter kept the exterior washed and waxed and the interior spotless as a matter of course. "My clients deserve to be pampered when I take them to see properties," he had told her when they worked together on Rockdale High's tenth reunion. As a gag, the reunion committee presented Walter with a special award for owning the largest automobile in their graduating class. He had accepted it with his perennial smile, but when someone asked him what he would do with the award, his expression turned serious. "I'm going to frame it, since it's the only kind of award

I ever got from Rockdale High School."

Now, as Walter unlocked the car doors and helped Mary in, she asked him about it. "Did you keep the certificate the committee gave you for having the largest car at the tenth reunion?"

Walter's smile deepened. "Sure do. In fact, it's hanging in my office, between my brokers' license and Better Business Bureau membership plaque. Like I said, I'm ready for another reunion."

"And I'm still not rested up from the first one."

Walter turned his car onto Main Street. "I'm glad you came with me."

"I still don't know where I'm going."

"To see a piece of land that might be on the market soon."

"Why?" Mary asked. "I'm not interesting in buying property."

"Maybe you should be. Land can be a great investment, you know."

Mary laughed. "My teacher's salary doesn't give me much extra money to invest."

"You and the judge could go in on it together."

"Go in on what?" Mary made no effort to mask the irritation she was beginning to feel.

"You'll see," he said.

Mary felt a touch of déjà vu at his words, so much like what Todd Walker had said the day before. For a moment, she wondered if Walter would also take her to the Millican bluff land. However, he'd told Ellie he'd be back at his office in thirty minutes, so they weren't going far.

Walter stopped at a traffic light at the precise moment Sally Proffitt emerged from the Clip and Curl Beauty Shop, where she had a standing Wednesday morning appointment. Jenny Suiter also had her hair done there by a different operator on Friday morning. Mary suspected the women compared notes on what each heard, but she doubted if they received more news than they imparted. In Mary's opinion, it was more blessed neither to give nor receive gossip, but apparently Sally

Proffitt and Jenny Suiter thought it their Christian duty to share "news."

Sally saw Mary immediately. She must have recognized the car—Walter Chance had the only one exactly like it in Rockdale. She looked surprised, then smiled and waved at Mary, who nodded in greeting.

"Too bad you don't have tinted side windows," Mary told Walter when the light turned green.

"Why?" Since Walter obviously hadn't seen Sally Proffitt, she decided not to tell him. *Do not worry about tomorrow. . . . Each day has enough trouble of its own.* Of course, Sally had nothing to tell the town; the fact that Mary Oliver and Walter Chance happened to be in the same vehicle on a sunny mid-morning in June could hardly be headline news, even in sensation-deprived Rockdale.

"It would make the interior cooler," she said.

"I can crank up the air conditioning." Walter reached out to change the temperature setting, but Mary stayed his hand.

"It's fine like it is."

"If you get uncomfortable, let me know."

The only thing I'm uncomfortable about is riding off to parts unknown with you. "I will."

"You probably know where we're headed by now," Walter said when he turned onto the narrow road leading to Oliver Mountain.

"Yes, but I don't know why. The only thing up here is our family's cemetery, and it isn't for sale."

Walter smiled faintly. "I didn't think it was."

He drove past the entrance to the cemetery and onto an even narrower unpaved lane, which ended abruptly at a grassy meadow. "Here we are," he announced.

Mary got out of the car, aware she wasn't dressed for hiking. She wasn't wearing a hat, so she risked further sunburn. Once again, her open-toed sandals weren't meant for uncertain terrain. Mary's slacks and knit top were more practical than yesterday's linen suit, but they offered no protection against the chigoes lurking in the weeds at the edge of the meadow. Unless Mary took precautions against the tiny pests, they delighted in burrowing into her skin, leaving red, itching welts all over her body.

Walter handed Mary a can of insecticide. "Spray this around your feet and ankles and on your arms. There are chiggers up here."

"I know. Thanks—I don't enjoy being eaten alive."

"I always carry bug spray," Walter said. "It comes in handy when I show rural property."

"I don't understand why you brought me here."

"You will."

Mystified, Mary followed Walter through a patch of weeds at the edge of the meadow and onto a rock outcropping overlooking Rockdale. The view, while not nearly so spectacular as the one Mary had seen at Millican's Bluff the day before, was impressive.

"A lot of people would think this is an ideal place to build a house."

A lot of people? Or Walter Chance?

Mary turned her head and glanced in the direction of the cemetery. "At least their neighbors won't be having any late-night parties."

Walter seemed slightly shocked Mary would speak so lightly of the last resting places of so many of her ancestors. "You wouldn't mind living up here? Many people wouldn't want a house close to a cemetery."

Mary spoke more seriously. "Maybe they don't want to be reminded of their own mortality. My eternal home is elsewhere, so cemeteries don't make me feel uncomfortable—especially not my own family's burial place."

"I know a contractor who could really build a fine house up here."

"Are you trying to tell me you want to build a house on our mountain?"

"No. This bluff land is far too valuable for a single home."

Mary felt the familiar irritation with Walter she'd encountered when they worked on their class reunion. Sometimes he could be downright—she searched for the right word—*frustrating.* "Do you mean someone wants to develop a whole subdivision up here?"

"No. Something much more profitable." Walter bent to scoop up a handful of loose stones from the rocks around them. "See this? Oliver Mountain is almost solid rock. That's unusual, because most of the ranges around here are riddled with limestone caves."

"Like Sequoyah Caverns," said Mary, who had recently gone there to arrange the Vacation Bible School field trip.

"Right. What we have here is a perfect location for a rock quarry."

eleven

A rock quarry?

Mary had seen enough rock quarries to know they were unsightly. A quarry on the brow of Oliver Mountain would be fully visible to at least half of Rockdale, an ugly scar on the otherwise green landscape. "You believe someone plans to put a rock quarry in here?"

"I don't know for sure, but it's a pretty good guess."

Mary thought of the noise and dust a working rock quarry would generate only yards from her family's cemetery. "That would be awful. Does the Civic Improvement Association know about this?"

Walter tossed the pebbles out and over the edge of the hill and dusted his hands on the sides of his slacks. "No. I heard someone from out of town ordered a geological survey, but I don't know who, and I don't know who did the work. It's all based on rumor, but I thought the judge might want to look into it."

"I'm sure he will. I'll tell him." Mary took one last look around the peaceful Oliver Mountain meadow and shuddered at the thought it might eventually be whittled away to nothing. "A quarry here would be terrible."

Walter nodded. "To prevent that, this land should be zoned for single-family dwellings only. That would be a good thing for the Civic Improvement Association to look into. It could be their first accomplishment."

"I'm sure my father will want to look into it right away."

Mary turned to go back to the car, but Walter caught her hand and stopped her. "I wanted to see you today for another reason. I want to take you out to dinner tonight—your necklace will look really great with the dress you wore to your birthday dinner. How about it?"

Caught off guard, Mary glanced at her watch as if the present time had any bearing on his invitation. "Uh—this is Wednesday. Father and I have a standing dinner engagement at the First Church fellowship supper."

Walter released Mary's hand. "How about tomorrow night, then?"

Mary looked into his eyes and knew she had to tell Walter the truth. "There's something you need to know—I won't ever be wearing the necklace."

He looked bewildered. "Why not?"

Mary took a deep breath and looked heavenward as if for guidance. "I can't. I don't have it anymore. I put it in a manila envelope and left it at your office yesterday. It's probably still on your desk."

"Why did you do that? I thought you liked it."

"My father and I agree it's too expensive for me to accept."

"The judge told you to give it back?"

"No, but—"

"Don't worry about the money—I can afford it. I just wanted you to have something as special as you are."

Walter looked unhappy, and Mary spoke quickly. "I'm not that special. And I want you to know I appreciate it—and your friendship—more than I can say."

His face brightened. "Then you'll wear it when we go out tomorrow night?"

"No—anyway, I never said I'd go with you."

"Forget the necklace. I don't care if you wear it or not, I'm still taking you somewhere nice tomorrow night."

Confronted with a combination of Walter's determination and her own wish to spare his feelings, Mary nodded. "If you insist."

Walter smiled. "I'll look at tomorrow's appointments and let you know what time I can pick you up."

Back in town, Walter stopped his car in the street behind her Toyota. No one was around to see her get out of Walter's car, but Mary figured the harm was already done. Sally Proffitt had probably already told the world that Judge Oliver's daughter, who had been seen riding in a red convertible with one man, was now riding around with Walter Chance.

&

When Mary got home, she left a message for her father to call her when he had the chance. She was preparing a salad for her lunch when he returned her call.

"What's up?"

"I ran into Walter today. He's heard something about Oliver Mountain you should know."

Mary repeated Walter's news without adding he had taken her to the site. "He said he didn't mention it to anyone on the Civic Improvement Association because it was hearsay, but he thought you'd want to follow up on it."

"This is disturbing—I'm glad you didn't wait to tell me. I'll see if I can find out who requested that geological survey. There won't be a quarry on that mountain, I can assure you."

"I hope not."

"Since you've seen Walter, I presume he knows you returned the necklace. How did he take it?"

"Not very well. I agreed to have dinner with him tomorrow night, and that seemed to make him feel better."

Mary sensed her father's smile. "I'm sure it did. I'll try to track down that survey after court adjourns, but it might take awhile. If I'm not home by five-thirty, go to the church supper without me. I'll try to get there before the serving line closes."

"I hope you can find the information," Mary said.

"So do I. See you later, puddin'."

Puddin'—her father hadn't called Mary by her childhood nickname in years. *He's getting mellower with every passing day.*

Mary believed the change in her father could be summed up in two words: Evelyn Trent—and she would be at the church supper that night, too.

&

Mary and her father seldom missed First's Wednesday night

fellowship dinner. For Mary, it was a midweek break from cooking, and her father enjoyed being with his friends. Even when they arrived together, Mary and Judge Oliver usually sat at separate tables. On this night, when her father still hadn't come home by nearly six o'clock, Mary followed his instruction and went by herself.

After Mary came through the serving line, Jennifer Stokes invited her to sit with her and her husband at one end of the long table. Their children sat at the other end, as far away as they could get. Mary had scarcely put down her tray before Alice Taylor and her children joined them.

"Here come the Smiths," Jennifer said. "We could have a Vacation Bible School committee meeting on the spot."

"Count us men out of that, please," Dub Taylor said.

"Ron is helping Melanie with the recreation this year. You could give us some of your time, too," Jennifer said.

"Alice spends enough hours at church for both of us," said Dub Taylor.

Mary listened to the couples' good-natured banter as an outsider, glimpsing things she'd never experienced and therefore could never fully understand. Still, she thanked God for Christian friends who laughed with her, not at her.

When Mary returned to the table with her ice water, the adults at the table suddenly fell silent. Mary immediately assumed she was the topic of their conversation. *Sally Proffitt must have struck again.*

"What were you talking about?"

Alice and Jennifer exchanged a quick glance. "We were checking out the judge," Jennifer said.

Mary hadn't seen her father enter, and when she automatically glanced at the table he usually shared with a few old friends, she saw he wasn't among them. Jennifer pointed toward a rear table, where Wayne Oliver sat with his back to the rest of the diners.

He wasn't alone: Evelyn Trent, whose distinctive silver hair stood out in any crowd, sat beside him. They seemed to be deep in conversation, apparently oblivious to the rest of the world.

Mary smiled faintly. "My father told me to come on by myself because he might be late."

"Now we know why," Jennifer said.

Her tone made Mary feel she should defend him. "He had to work late. Besides, he and Evelyn Trent have been friends for years."

"True, but they never seemed to be quite *this* friendly," Alice said.

"You sound like Sally Proffitt," said Melanie.

Alice made a face. "Well, Miss Sally isn't here tonight, so somebody has to do her job."

They were all smiling, and Mary was glad no one seemed to expect her to say anything else about her father and the retired social worker. Mary thought of telling them she and Walter Chance were going out the next evening. That would change the subject in a hurry, but Mary remained silent.

"If women's gossip could be taxed, this town would have all the money it could use," Dub Taylor said.

"Women aren't the only ones who like to talk," Alice retorted. "What about all those stories you guys like to tell about the fish that got away and how many holes below par you shot playing golf?"

"Men talk about things of interest. We don't talk about other people behind their backs," Dub said.

"I'll remind you of that the next time you start discussing the mill manager," Alice said.

"Hey, that's not gossip—that's reporting facts."

Everyone laughed, but in a way, Dub's words hit the mark. Sally Proffitt and Jenny Suiter too often reached completely wrong conclusions about the "facts" they reported.

Mary hoped Sally Proffitt wouldn't be on her front porch when Walter came to pick her up.

❧

The families at Mary's table gradually drifted away, the adults to the sanctuary for the midweek service and the children to their special activities. Among the last to leave the fellowship hall, Wayne Oliver and Evelyn Trent joined Mary in the hallway outside the sanctuary.

"Did you find the information you were looking for?" Mary asked her father.

"Not yet. The firms doing that work are scattered all over and many are one-man operations with answering machines. I meant to get home earlier, but as I told Evelyn, the time got away from me."

"I ran late tonight myself," Evelyn said.

"We were talking about the Rockdale Civic Improvement Association meeting," her father said, as if Mary had asked.

Mary didn't try to suppress her smile. "That must have been fascinating dinner conversation."

Evelyn nodded. "Actually, it was. He's trying to persuade me to join the steering committee."

"You should. You know everybody in Rock County."

"I did in the past, but I've been out of town so much since I retired, I'm behind the times."

"Rockdale still moves in the slow lane," Mary said. "You haven't missed much."

"So Wayne tells me."

When the first piano chords signaled the start of the service, Wayne Oliver led the way to the family pew. Seated between Mary and Evelyn, Mary's father handed her a hymnal and shared another with Evelyn. As they sang, Mary noticed he stood closer to Evelyn than hymnal sharing required.

Watching them, Mary felt a lump rise in her throat. Her father and Evelyn looked completely at ease with each other. *This the way it's going to be from now on. It's only a matter of time until they marry. After that, our lives will never be the same again.*

Even without that prospect, Mary hardly knew how to handle the changes in her own life.

As Dr. Whitson led in prayer, Mary silently raised her own petition. *I thank You for bringing my father and Evelyn together,*

Lord. Help me to accept the changes going on around me. Help me live constantly in Your will, not mine.

When Mary opened her eyes, Evelyn looked at her as if she knew something of Mary's inner struggle and felt sympathy for her.

Evelyn Trent could become my stepmother. Mary tested the thought and found it was not at all unpleasant. She smiled at Evelyn, who smiled back.

Her father looked puzzled. "Why are you two smiling? Did I miss something?" he whispered.

"It's just a girl thing," Mary whispered back. At that, Evelyn bent her head and covered her mouth, her shoulders shaking in silent laughter.

Looking baffled, he muttered "Women!" under his breath, and Mary almost laughed aloud. Fortunately, the choir director announced another hymn, and somewhere during the second verse, she and Evelyn managed to regain their composure.

❧

After the benediction, Evelyn and her father left together, headed for the side lot where both had parked their cars, and Mary drove home from church alone. She was reading the newspaper in the living room when her father came in almost an hour later.

"You and Evelyn seemed to be having a good time tonight," he said. "What was that all about?"

"I believe Evelyn and I reached an understanding tonight. I wonder if you have."

Wayne Oliver looked mystified. "What do you mean?"

"How do you feel about Evelyn?"

He smiled ruefully. "It seems we've had this conversation before. We're very good friends, and I can assure you my intentions are honorable."

"If you're going to marry her, I'd rather hear it from you than get a garbled version from Sally Proffitt or Jenny Suiter."

"Those gossips! You can't believe anything they say."

"I don't—that's why I'm asking you."

"Evelyn and I enjoy each other's company. At first, the thought of a more permanent arrangement never entered my mind, and I'm sure she felt the same way. Evelyn's never been married, and she's used to being independent. So am I. But lately, we've grown closer. . . ."

When her father didn't finish his thought, Mary went over to his chair and gave him a brief hug. "I believe you should ask Evelyn to be your wife."

He looked uncertain. "You wouldn't mind?"

"How could I? It's obvious you're happy when you're together."

He looked relieved. "You don't know how much I've prayed about this. I'm not sure Evelyn will have me, but knowing you approve makes it easier to ask her."

"Be assured you have my blessing."

Her father's voice was husky with emotion. "Thank you, my dear. I only hope you'll know such happiness one day."

"I haven't been looking for it."

"Neither were Evelyn and I. Things change—we go along in the same rut for years, then the Lord moves us in an entirely different direction. When that happens to you, I trust you'll recognize it."

I think I am beginning to. "When, not if?" Mary questioned.

"When," he repeated. "I believe you're close to realizing I need some grandchildren."

Mary smiled, but she recognized the truth in her father's words. She had always assumed she would cook and keep house for her father as long as he lived. It had never occurred to her that he wished for grandchildren. He had never spoken of it, probably because it seemed so unlikely Mary would ever marry.

"I'll see what I can do about that one of these days," Mary said. "For now, I'm going to bed."

Late into the night, Mary considered the uncertain future ahead when her father and Evelyn married.

They'll have to live here—Evelyn's house is far too small. She'll want to bring some of her furniture and personal items, and that means rearranging everything.

Mary sighed. She believed God had a solution for every one of her problems. Now she prayed to find them.

twelve

Her father came down for breakfast Thursday morning, humming and smelling of aftershave lotion.

"Beautiful morning, isn't it?"

Mary smiled at his good humor. "You probably don't care, but the weather forecast mentions scattered thunderstorms and heavy rain this afternoon. You'd better take your umbrella."

"Maybe the storms will be scattered somewhere else. Anyway, I'll be inside all day. This afternoon I hope to find out who tested land on our mountain. I'm glad Walter told you about it when he did."

"Remember I'm having dinner with him tonight, so I won't be here when you get home."

"Where's he taking you?"

"I don't know—out of town, though. He said he'll let me know later today when he can get away to pick me up."

Her father smiled. "Should I wait up for you tonight?"

"Hardly. Even if we go to Mentone, we should be back by nine."

"Ask Walter in when you get home. I'd like to discuss this quarry business with him."

"Maybe you should go with us." Mary could imagine the look on Walter Chance's face if her father did so.

"No, thanks. Three's a crowd."

❧

Walter called Mary shortly after noon. "Was the judge able to find out who owns the land on Oliver Mountain?" he asked.

"Not yet, but he's working on it."

"Good. I'll pick you up at five-thirty."

The weather was fine when Walter called, but by five o'clock, the earlier sunny skies had been replaced by billowing thunderclouds, and the scent of rain hung heavy in the air.

Mary put on her red linen suit, then rummaged in the coat closet for her ancient black nylon taffeta raincoat. It wasn't glamorous, but Mary was more interested in keeping dry.

Walter rang the doorbell promptly at the appointed hour. "I'm sorry I didn't bring better weather, but I see you're prepared for the worst," he said when she opened the door.

"I call this raincoat 'Old Faithful'—I think I've had it since tenth grade."

"It still looks very nice—and so do you."

Walter had exchanged his usual casual attire for the kind of ensemble featured in department store ads. His beige sport coat, navy blue slacks, pale blue dress shirt, and beige and navy patterned tie looked new, and Mary caught the subtle scent of a spicy aftershave.

He must have shaved and changed clothes after work. The knowledge both unsettled and touched Mary, and she wished he wouldn't try so hard to impress her.

Thunder growled in the distance, and when they reached Walter's car, Mary glanced across the street. The empty front porch swing moved slightly in the rising wind, and the drapes at the front windows were closed. Mary was grateful Sally Proffitt wouldn't see Walter help her into his Towncar.

"I wanted to take you someplace better," Walter said as they headed out of town, "but with all the bad weather, I thought we should settle for DeSoto Park. Is that all right?"

"Of course. I haven't eaten there at night in a long time."

"The buffet is usually good, but we can order from the menu if you don't like what they have tonight."

Walter's obvious eagerness to please made Mary feel even worse. "Let's decide when we get there."

He nodded as if she had said something profound. "Good idea—but then, you always have good ideas. That's one of the many things I like about you."

"Here comes the rain," Mary said a moment later. A few dime-sized drops pelted the windshield, soon joined by hundreds of others in a sky-wide curtain.

Walter wasn't driving fast before the rain began, but now he slowed even more and turned on the car's headlights. Even at high speed, the windshield wipers were unable to keep up with the increasing volume of rain.

I hope Walter can see the road better than I can. Mary almost told him so, but she didn't want to break his concentration.

Mary peered out at the sky, a uniform dark gray as far as she could see. A bolt of lightning cut through the air nearby, followed almost at once by a tremendous thunderclap. Startled, she shivered. "That sounded like a sonic boom."

"Don't worry—a car like this is about the safest place you can be in a storm."

"I'm not worried." Afraid she had spoken too sharply, Mary tried to make amends. "You're a good driver."

Walter smiled at her compliment. "I try to drive safely all the time, of course, but especially when I carry such precious cargo."

Mary manufactured a sudden cough to cover her reaction. *Precious cargo, indeed! At least he didn't put one of those 'Baby on Board' signs in the rear window.* Walter's attempt at being gallant made her feel almost sorry for him.

Mary's fake coughing fit did not go unnoticed. "I keep a package of lozenges in the glove box. Help yourself."

She tried to look grateful and went through the motions of unwrapping one of the red disks without putting it in her mouth.

"All better?" Walter asked in a moment, and she nodded. "Yes, thank you."

Mary sighed and glanced at her wristwatch. She had been with Walter fifteen minutes, yet it had already been a long evening.

❧

Mary hoped the storm would be spent by the time they reached the park, but the rain seemed to have followed them there, then increased in intensity.

Walter reached behind the driver's seat for the largest umbrella Mary had ever seen. "I came prepared. This will keep us dry."

As he spoke, lightning flashed again, followed closely by rolling thunder. Mary had never feared storms, but she flinched at the sudden noise. "Let's wait awhile. We didn't come all the way up here to be struck by lightning."

Walter laughed as if Mary had said something hilarious. "I've always enjoyed your sly sense of humor."

"You're only saying that because it's true," she said lightly.

This time, Walter didn't return her smile. "I mean it, Mary. I'm just not very good at this."

He spoke with great sincerity and reached for Mary's hand.

Afraid he would try to kiss her, Mary reclaimed her hand and pulled up her raincoat hood. "The lightning seems to be letting up. It's probably safe to go inside."

"If you say so. Stay right there."

Walter got out of the car and opened his black umbrella, on which CHANCE REALTY was printed in large red letters. He helped Mary out and put his arm around her on the pretext of sheltering her under his umbrella. He kept a firm hold on her all the way to the DeSoto Park Lodge porch, and when he finally let her go to close the umbrella, he seemed to do so reluctantly.

He smiled. "That wasn't so bad, was it?"

It depends on what you mean. I could certainly have done without being hugged quite so much. "No. The umbrella kept me dry."

"Remind me to give you one. I keep a few in the car in case I have to show property in the rain."

Walter put his hand on the small of Mary's back and steered her into the dining area as if she couldn't find the way unassisted. Even though Walter was trying to be polite, the gesture embarrassed her.

Mary recognized the hostess, a senior the year she and Walter entered Rockdale High School. *Sally something*—Mary couldn't think of her last name.

"Good evening, Walter—hi, Mary—I guess y'all are dining together tonight?"

"Hello, Sally. We sure are, and I hope you have a nice, quiet table away from the traffic."

"There might not be much of that tonight, the way it's storming. I can seat you by a window if you like."

Walter looked at Mary. "How about it? Do you want to watch the rain?"

"No. I teach my first-graders to stay away from windows during a storm."

"Then I reckon we should, too," Walter said.

"Follow me." The hostess led them to a table tucked away in a corner, far from the windows. "Do you need a menu?"

"How about it, Mary?"

"The buffet will be fine."

"Two buffets, then? Your waitress will take your drink orders. Enjoy your meal."

"Sally Richmond," Mary said when the hostess walked away.

"What?"

"The hostess—her name is Sally Richmond."

"Was," Walter corrected. "She's married to Ted Morgan. I sold them a house near Warren Mountain a couple of years ago. In fact, it's in Toni and David Trent's neighborhood."

They fell silent again as the storm continued to rage. Lightning flashed almost constantly, accompanied by booming thunder. The dining room lights flickered a few times but never went out.

"I sure picked a terrible time to take you out," Walter said after an especially loud burst of thunder shook the building.

He sounded so forlorn Mary tried to cheer him up. "This is a typical summer storm—it won't last long, and the rest of the evening will probably be fine."

The waitress arrived at their table before Walter had time to reply. "What can I get y'all to drink this evening?"

He answered without consulting Mary. "I'll take sweetened

iced tea, and the lady will have ice water with a slice of lemon."

"How did you know that's what I wanted?" Mary asked when the waitress left.

"Easy. All those times the reunion committee met at Statum's, you always ordered water with lemon. You did it the other day, too."

"You have a good memory."

"It's good to remember the good times, but making happy new memories together is even better."

Mary began another effort to tell Walter not to read too much into her reasons for going out with him. "You really shouldn't—"

With uncanny timing, the waitress brought their drinks. "Here you are. Feel free to go to the buffet any time, and let me know if you need anything else."

Walter smiled. "How about it? I don't know about you, but I'm ready to tie on the old feed bag."

The old feed bag? Mary sighed. It seemed every time Mary began to feel closer to Walter, he managed to say or do something odd.

"Fine," she said aloud. "Lead the way."

❧

Mary's weather prediction proved correct. While they were eating, the black storm clouds moved on and the sun came out again. Walter's mood lightened, and he began to talk about all the good things he hoped the Rockdale Civic Improvement Association would be able to bring about for the community.

"I might even run for city council if that's what it takes to get better zoning laws."

"Since you're in the real estate business, some people might see that as a conflict of interest. You could do more good working behind the scenes."

Walter nodded. "You're right—I hadn't thought of that. Somebody needs to step up to the plate and wake up the powers that be, or there's no telling what kind of mess Rockdale will wind up in. The quarry is just the tip of the iceberg."

"That reminds me—my father wants to talk to you about it tonight."

"I figured he would, but I hadn't planned to end this evening in Judge Oliver's company."

Mary wasn't sure she wanted to know what else Walter might have preferred, and she didn't ask.

Walter apparently took her silence to mean agreement. "Don't worry, we'll have lots of other evenings together."

Don't take that for granted, Mary almost blurted out, but Walter's expression made her soften her words.

"I've enjoyed dinner tonight, I really have. You're a very special friend, but that's all."

Walter seemed amused. "Don't be so serious. Being good friends was a good start for us, but it surely won't be the end."

Mary felt frustrated. Walter almost seemed to think she was playing hard to get. While she suspected nothing she could say would change his mind, Mary had to try. "In this case, I think it is."

To her chagrin, Walter smiled. "There's that dry sense of humor again. You're something else, Mary Oliver."

"So are you," Mary retorted, and he laughed aloud.

When the waitress removed their plates, Walter glanced at his watch. "We have time to walk down to the waterfall, if you'd like to do that now."

Mary shook her head, glad for a ready excuse. "The path will be slippery after all the rain, and I'm not wearing my hiking shoes."

"Of course—I wasn't thinking. I certainly don't want to do anything to cause you harm."

"Thanks," Mary said quickly. "Maybe we should get back to Rockdale now."

Walter flashed a big smile. "Your wish is my command, milady."

Stifling a sigh, Mary allowed Walter to steer her from the dining room.

thirteen

They reached Mary's house shortly after eight o'clock, and her father quickly invited Walter inside.

"I've made several inquiries, but no one seems to know anything about a geological survey on Oliver Mountain," he told Walter. "I want to know exactly what you heard."

"It's all second hand, but I have a few ideas about it and some other things, too."

"Sit down and tell me about it."

Walter did, and for a while, Mary feared he and her father would talk all night.

A half hour into their discussion, she made some coffee and heated a plate of brownies she'd frozen after Decoration Day.

"These taste like you just baked them," Walter declared. "You sure know your way around a kitchen."

"That she does," Mary's father agreed. "Have another brownie."

Mary rolled her eyes and retreated to her room to read.

Walter finally left shortly before the ten o'clock news, which Mary and her father had watched together for years. She was putting their cups into the dishwasher when he came into the kitchen.

"Walter said something interesting while you were out of the room."

"What was that?"

Mary's father leaned against the kitchen counter and folded his arms across his chest. "Mr. Chance seems unwilling to take 'no' for an answer. He wants me to use my influence to persuade you to keep the necklace."

"I thought we agreed I shouldn't."

"Maybe it wouldn't be such a bad idea. Walter assured me he can afford it."

"I don't care. It's not the kind of gift one accepts from a friend."

"Surely you know he wants to be more than that."

Mary closed the dishwasher. "Is that what he told you?"

He laughed. "You two remind me of eighth graders in the throes of a first crush. They can't talk to each other, so they have to let their friends talk for them."

"Believe me, I don't have a crush on Walter Chance."

"That's too bad. He all but asked me for your hand."

Mary studied her father's face and decided he was serious. "What did you tell him?"

"The truth. My daughter has a mind of her own, and I have nothing to do with her love life."

Mary didn't know whether to laugh or cry. "My love life! Please tell me you didn't use those words."

"Walter wants to be your personal Prince Charming. He's a nice fellow—if you can't love him, try not to break his heart."

ఎ

Mary wasn't surprised when Walter called the next morning to tell her how much he'd enjoyed going out with her. When he asked her to have lunch with him, she quickly refused.

"I can't."

"If you change your mind—"

"I won't."

Mary could picture Walter's baffled shrug. "Okay. See you later."

Being pursued was new to her, but Mary hoped Walter would soon realize she had no interest in being caught.

She had no sooner hung up than the telephone rang again. Thinking it might be Walter calling her back, Mary took her time answering.

"Mary Oliver? This is Jason Abbott."

Jason Abbott. Her heart lurched unaccountably, and she

realized she'd been hoping he'd call. "Yes?"

"We met Monday at DeSoto State Park, and you were kind enough to offer to tell me about your children's programs."

"Yes, I remember."

"When would it be convenient for us to meet?"

"Do you have a specific time in mind?"

"I'm free the rest of today and tomorrow. After that, it would be sometime next week before we could get together."

"Around two this afternoon is fine for me."

"Good. I'd like to see First's facilities, if that's possible."

"I'll be happy to give you a tour. I can meet you in front of the sanctuary—it's on Spring Street."

"I know. Pastor Hurley pointed it out when we toured Rockdale."

Mary smiled at the thought of "touring" such a small town. *That must have taken all of a half hour.* "I'll see you there at two o'clock."

❧

The courthouse clock had just struck twice when Mary pulled into her usual parking place at the side of First Church. While she was unfastening her safety belt, a dark green Honda sedan pulled up beside her. A man wearing jeans, a knit shirt, and white athletic shoes got out and approached her. His hair looked freshly cut, and Mary suspected he had shaved that morning, but he still looked slightly shaggy.

"Thanks for agreeing to meet with me."

"I'm always glad to talk about our children's department. We've put a lot of work into it."

Jason followed Mary through the double front doors and pushed his sunglasses to the top of his head. Once inside the sanctuary, Jason stopped to look at the stained glass windows. The afternoon sun streamed through them, casting multicolored beams of light across the pews.

"I wondered if the inside of this church could be as beautiful as the outside. Now I see it is. That's a great-looking pipe organ. Is it still used?"

"Every Sunday. The walls shake when Mrs. Harvey pulls out all the stops."

"I can imagine." Jason glanced at the walls on either side. "These stained glass windows are extraordinary."

"Most of them date back to the late eighteen hundreds," Mary said.

"You can tell they were made with great care by a master craftsman." Jason walked around the pews to get a closer look at the western windows. "This one of Jesus with the children is superb."

"It's my favorite," Mary said.

Jason bent to read the placard beneath the window, then looked at Mary. "Are you related to the Olivers who commissioned this window?"

"Yes, and my mother's family gave the one beside it."

"It's beautiful, but I prefer the Oliver window. That one little girl looks as if she could step right out of the scene at any moment."

"She wouldn't want to, though. She would have stayed at the Master's side."

"Those who come to Jesus as children usually stay with Him their entire lives. That's why I want Community Church to introduce as many children to Christ as possible."

"We try to do that here, too."

They stood looking at the windows in companionable silence a few moments longer, then Jason spoke. "I could stay here all afternoon, but I suppose we should move on."

Mary led Jason from the sanctuary into the administrative area. "I would introduce you to Dr. Whitson, but our pastor leaves at noon on Fridays to work on his Sunday sermon."

"I expect we'll meet at the Rock County Ministerial Association dinner later this month."

Next, Mary led Jason into the children's area of the educational wing, stopping to explain each area. As they went, he took notes and asked a few questions.

"These are the preschool and kindergarten classes. The

youth painted the wall murals over the last few summers. The work gave those who weren't helping with Vacation Bible School something positive to do."

"Good idea. You don't have a day care program?"

"No. We don't really have anywhere to put one."

"I'd like to start one at Community. What about after-school programs?"

"Some of our kids come for one-on-one tutoring a few times a week during the school year, and volunteers open the church library from time to time in the summer."

"Programs like that can be a great outreach." Jason Abbott replaced his notebook in his shirt pocket, and Mary assumed he had all the information he wanted.

"Is there anything else you want to know?"

"I don't want to be a pest, but I understand you're doing something different for Vacation Bible School. Can you tell me a little about it?"

"Sure, but all the material is at my house. If you like, you can follow me home."

Jason Abbott's sudden smile transformed his unremarkable features. "Like a stray dog? If it's not convenient, just say so. I don't want to impose on you."

"You're not. Besides, I'd like your opinion of what we're doing."

"Since you put it that way, lead on, Miss Oliver."

"The children call me Miss Mary, but for you, Mary will do."

"I've been known as Brother Jason, Pastor Jason, and Pastor Abbott, but to my friends, I'm just Jason—and I'd like you to call me that, too."

"All right, Jason. We can go out this side door by the office."

&

Instead of turning into the Oliver driveway, Mary stopped in front of the house. Seeing Sally Proffitt sitting on her front porch, Mary waved to her.

"I want you to meet my neighbor," Mary told Jason, and

they walked across the street together.

Sally Proffitt stood, obviously curious about the strange man with Mary Oliver.

"Mrs. Proffitt, I'd like you to meet Jason Abbott. He's the new associate pastor at Community Church, and he's coming to my house to see the materials we're using at our Vacation Bible School this year."

Jason smiled and extended his hand. "I'm pleased to meet you, Mrs. Proffitt. You look like someone with Vacation Bible School experience yourself."

Sally Proffitt looked pleased. "In my time I worked with little ones, but my arthritis got so bad I had to give it up."

Jason looked sympathetic. "Being with children is such a blessing, I know you must miss it."

For once, Sally Proffitt had nothing to say, and Mary took advantage of her silence. "Maybe you and Mrs. Suiter will consider helping us with the VBS refreshments this year," Mary said.

Sally Proffitt looked embarrassed. "We'll think about it."

Mary and Jason went back across the street to the Oliver house, leaving an obviously deflated woman behind.

"What was that all about?" Jason asked when Mary stopped to unlock the front door.

"I wanted Mrs. Proffitt to meet you. Otherwise, she would have wondered why you were here."

Jason smiled. "I know women like her. Every place has a few."

Mary decided to say nothing more about her nosy neighbor as they entered the house, dim and blessedly cool in the mid-afternoon heat.

Jason Abbott looked around. "I love your house. They don't make them like this anymore."

"If you saw the utility bills, you might understand why. We'll sit at the dining room table, where there's room to spread out the materials."

Mary excused herself to get her folders, then she stopped

by the kitchen and returned with a tray bearing a pitcher of lemonade and a plate with the remaining brownies.

"You shouldn't have gone to all this trouble," Jason said when she put the tray on the table.

"I didn't. I made the lemonade at lunch, and the brownies were on hand."

Jason bit into one. "Umm, a homemade brownie. This is a real treat."

The way to a man's heart is through his stomach. Mary didn't know why the old saying had popped into her mind. She took it for granted that a man like Jason Abbott was already taken, so they could have no more than a shared professional interest.

Mary sat down beside Jason and opened the first VBS folder. "Here's the schedule we plan to use."

Jason surveyed the stack of folders spread out before him. "This took a lot of work. I can tell you're an organized, can-do person."

"I didn't do it all by myself," Mary hastened to say. "My committee did much of the daily plans."

"Even so, someone has to take the lead. I hope to find some Mary Olivers at Community Church."

She smiled. "There's only one of me in Rockdale, but the Community congregation has many talented people who love the Lord."

Jason nodded. "So I'm told. Unfortunately, Mark Elliott went out of town about the time I got here and won't be back for a few weeks. It's hard to get the full picture of our children's programs without the education director."

"You must have many other things to do in the meantime," Mary said.

"Oh, yes—when I was interviewed, the personnel committee made it quite clear I'm expected to wear many hats. However, Pastor Hurley shares my heart for children, and meeting their needs will be a top priority."

"I believe God gave me a heart for children, too." Mary had

never said those words to anyone, yet she felt perfectly comfortable saying them to Jason Abbott.

He nodded. "That's obvious." He paused. "I'm glad He gave you the heart to help me, too."

fourteen

The hall clock was striking five when Jason Abbott stood to leave. Time had seemed to pass so quickly Mary was surprised to realize Jason had been there almost two hours.

"I didn't mean to spoil your entire afternoon," he said.

"You didn't. I enjoy talking shop."

At the door, Jason paused. "I hate to admit it, but I'm not sure how to get back to the Rockdale Inn."

"You're not living at the Oaks?"

"Not yet. I still have stuff to move from Georgia."

Mary gave Jason directions, and when he started down the walk, she noted Sally Proffitt watched him from her front porch. *No doubt she's timed every minute of Jason Abbott's visit.*

Jason pulled away from the curb seconds before Wayne Oliver's sedan turned into the driveway. Mary was collecting her VBS material when her father came into the dining room.

"Who was that?" he asked.

"Jason Abbott—the new associate pastor at Community. I was showing him our Vacation Bible School materials."

"Is he the one they're having a reception for Sunday afternoon?"

"Yes. From what I hear, they're looking forward to having him there."

Wayne Oliver glanced at his watch. "Shouldn't you be getting ready for that rehearsal dinner?"

Mary guessed the source of her father's concern. "Are you going out tonight, too?"

"Yes and no. Evelyn invited me to have supper at her house around six."

She smiled. "Tell her I said hello—and don't rush home on my account."

❧

Other than serving at the reception, Mary wasn't involved in Hawk Henson and Anita Sanchez's wedding, so at first she hadn't understood why Hawk Henson invited her to the rehearsal dinner. However, when he explained Anita Sanchez would have no family members there, she had agreed to fill in for them.

Told to dress casually, Mary chose a lime green pantsuit from her school wardrobe, paired with comfortable low-heeled shoes. Even though she knew no one would care what she wore, she added gold earrings. *As they should, all eyes will be on the happy bride.*

Mary had refused Hawk's offer to pick her up, preferring to drive herself. That way, she could come home whenever she liked. She had just arrived at Rockdale Country Club when a male voice called her name.

Jason Abbott had also changed his clothes. He now wore a light-colored sport jacket over a cotton dress shirt, and polished loafers had replaced his athletic shoes. He looked slightly rumpled, as if his clothes had been removed from a suitcase without being pressed.

"I didn't expect to see you tonight," Jason said. "I'm supposed to go to the Henson-Sanchez rehearsal dinner. How about you?"

"Me, too, although I'm not in the wedding."

"Neither am I, but something came up and Pastor Hurley asked me to take his place tonight. I haven't met either the bride or groom."

"You'll like them both," Mary said. "Anita Sanchez is originally from Colombia and she doesn't have any relatives here. Hawk Henson has a large family, and he invited me so she won't feel so outnumbered tonight."

"Thanks for the information. Shall we go inside?"

❧

When they reached the private dining room where the rehearsal dinner was being held, Mary found herself in the odd position of introducing Jason Abbott and Hawk Henson.

"Thanks for coming. Pastor Hurley told me you'd pinch-hit for him tonight." Hawk shook Jason's hand, then motioned for Anita to join them. "Anita, this is Pastor Jason Abbott."

She smiled and took his hand. "I am pleased to have the honor to meet you tonight, since Hawk and I will not be here Sunday afternoon for your reception."

"I won't ask why not," Jason said, and they smiled.

"Mary, you sit next to Toni," Hawk directed. "Pastor, you sit beside Mary and Anita. When my aunt and uncle arrive, I'll ask you to pray, then the food will be served."

Jason nodded. "Let me know when."

Mary greeted Toni, and they talked briefly about the *Record* article concerning the Rockdale Civic Improvement Association. After the last of his relatives arrived, Hawk introduced them to everyone, then announced Pastor Jason would offer an opening prayer.

Jason stood and thanked God for the food and the occasion and asked a special blessing on the couple who would be married the next day and on the home they would establish together.

"That was nice," Mary said when he sat down. "It wasn't long, yet it said exactly the right thing."

Jason looked amused. "Thanks. I'm glad you approved of my first official function on behalf of Community Church."

Mary realized she had seemed to critique his prayer. "I don't have a habit of judging public prayers. It's just that even though my pastor, Dr. Whitson, is a fine man and a wonderful preacher, he's given to rather long public prayers."

"I hate to interrupt you, but please pass the salad dressing," Toni Trent said.

Mary did so, and Jason turned away to talk to Anita Sanchez. "I went to Guatemala on a summer mission trip once," Mary heard him say, and later they exchanged a few sentences in Spanish.

"Our new associate pastor looks like a real winner," Toni told Mary. "We love Pastor Hurley, but it's good to have someone young enough to bring in new ideas."

Mary told Toni about Jason Abbott's visit to First Church to discuss children's programs.

"That's interesting," she said. "It's too bad Jason's engaged. He'd be perfect for you."

Engaged? Mary swallowed hard and hoped Jason hadn't overheard Toni's remark. "You sound like the other match-makers—you of all people should know better."

"I know David and I are blessed to be together. If God means for a match to be, it'll happen."

Jason turned back to Mary in time to hear the last part of Toni's statement. "What's going to happen?"

"The rehearsal," Mary said quickly.

Jason looked puzzled but didn't pursue the subject.

❧

"We're having a very simple wedding. I don't see why we need to rehearse," Hawk said when they entered the sanctuary.

"You need to know what to expect," said Toni, who served as the unofficial director. "You and Anita should be familiar with the music cues."

Mary settled into a pew to watch. After conferring with Toni, Janet Brown took her place at the electronic organ and played the final chords of a piece by Pachelbel, the signal for Jason Abbott, as Pastor Hurley, to emerge from a side door with David Trent, Hawk's best man.

Janet continued to play as little Juanita Sanchez walked in slowly, scattering pretend rose petals from the beribboned basket she'd use the next day. When Juanita reached the front, David had to remind her to take a few steps to the left and make a half turn before she stopped. When Toni came down the aisle next, David smiled as if remembering their wedding.

When Toni reached the altar and made her half turn, the organ struck the opening chords of the traditional music which launched tens of thousands of brides down thousands of church aisles annually. Mary, who was substituting for the mother of the bride, was the first to stand as Hawk and Anita entered together.

Mary's breath caught in her throat from the emotional impact of the love that shone so clearly from the couple's faces. When they reached the altar, Jason opened Pastor Hurley's book.

"Dearly beloved, we are gathered here," he began. Although he looked as if he'd like to continue, Jason stopped reading and addressed Hawk and Anita. "And so on."

After going through the ring ceremony, Jason told Anita and Hawk that Pastor Hurley would pronounce them husband and wife. "Then you'll turn and face the congregation."

"They have to kiss each other first," Toni said in a stage whisper, and everyone laughed.

"If you insist." Hawk barely brushed Anita's lips.

After another run-through with music, Toni decided they were ready for the real thing and reminded everyone what time they should gather at the church the next day.

"Thank you for filling in for Pastor Hurley," Toni told Jason. "Will you be at the wedding?"

"No. I have to go to Georgia to see about something."

Toni smiled. "Or someone? Anyway, you must be back for your reception on Sunday."

"Don't worry, I will."

Mary and Jason left the church at the same time and walked out into the soft summer night together.

"I'm sorry you'll miss the wedding," Mary said. "It should be a beautiful service."

"I know."

Mary was on the verge of asking Jason when he'd be rehearsing for his own wedding, but she didn't want to seem to pry. "I'll see you Sunday afternoon, then. Journey safe."

"Thanks. Good night, Mary."

On her way home, Mary realized she had enjoyed this

evening far more than she'd expected. Anita and Hawk practically glowed with their love, and so did Toni and David Trent. And, Mary supposed when she met Jason Abbott's fiancée, she'd see yet another devoted couple. *I am happy for them all, I really am.*

Why, then, should Mary suddenly feel so lonely?

❧

Compared to other weddings Mary had witnessed over the years, the Sanchez-Henson ceremony was small and simple, but it had a special charm. Anita looked beautiful in her ankle-length light yellow dress. Her short veil was attached to a headband covered with yellow roses, and Juanita performed her flower girl duties flawlessly. Hawk and Anita spoke their vows in strong voices, and even the sometimes tricky candle-lighting worked perfectly. Community Church was filled to capacity, and the guests burst into spontaneous applause when Ed Hurley introduced two previous individuals as Mr. and Mrs. Hawk Henson.

"What a lovely couple they make," said Phyllis Dickson, who had hired Anita to work at the Rockdale Hospital when she first came to town.

"That marriage was absolutely made in heaven," agreed Pastor Hurley's wife.

From her post at the serving table, Mary heard those comments and others like them. Many of the women had wept openly during the vows and their eyes were still red.

Walter Chance approached in his Sunday-best navy blue suit, smiling broadly. "Hello, Mary. You giving away that punch?"

Mary handed Walter a cup. "I didn't see you at the wedding."

"I was in the sniveling section on the groom's side. If weddings are supposed to be so wonderful, why do women cry?"

Mary smiled. "Not all do, but in many cases, I think it's an emotional reaction to the couple's happiness."

"Or maybe sadness because two more singles are no longer on the marriage market."

What marriage market? No such thing existed in Rockdale, but Mary would never say so to Walter.

He stepped aside to allow Mary to serve punch to others, then accepted a refill. "Since we're already dressed up, how about going to Mentone tonight? I still owe you a first-class dinner."

"You don't owe me anything, but I can't go in any case."

His face fell. "Previous plans?"

"You might say that." In a way, it was the truth—Mary had planned not to go out with Walter Chance again, at least not for a long time, and she steeled herself against his sad, lonely-Walter look.

"Oh, well, there'll always be another time," he said.

"Good-bye, Walter," Mary said pointedly, and he moved on.

Juanita Sanchez, still giddy from her performance as flower girl, held out her punch cup for a third refill. "Who was that man talking to you, Miss Mary?"

"Mr. Walter Chance. He has a real estate office."

Juanita looked disappointed. "I thought maybe he was the husman you wished for when you blew out your candles."

Mary tried not to laugh. "In the first place, I didn't wish for a *husband*. Besides, Mr. Chance and I are old friends."

Juanita didn't look convinced. "When you do get a husband, can I be your flower girl?"

Mary hugged the little girl. "You were wonderful today, and I can't think of anyone I'd rather have as my flower girl."

Juanita's dark eyes shone with pleasure. "Really?"

"Really. But let's keep that our secret, shall we?"

Juanita nodded solemnly. "All right, Miss Mary. I won't even tell Jackie Tate, and you know she's my bestest friend."

A commotion at the other end of the hall signaled Hawk and Anita's approaching departure, and Toni Trent came over to head Mary and Juanita in that direction.

"Hurry up, Juanita, so you can see your mother throw her bouquet."

Mary had never tried to catch a bride's bouquet, and she

didn't intend to start now. She stopped at the edge of the half circle of young women whose arms were stretched out to Anita. Once, twice, and a third time, the bride made as if she would throw her bridal bouquet but did not. Then, as the women were laughing and out of position, she tossed it up and over them in a perfect arc.

Mary saw it coming toward her, and when she raised her arms in self-defense, the bouquet flew into them.

Everyone cheered and clapped when they saw who had caught the bouquet. "Good for you, Mary Oliver!" someone cried out.

"There's Rockdale's next bride!" another declared.

Juanita beamed with pleasure. "See, Miss Mary! I knew you were going to get a husband."

"That's just an old tradition. It doesn't mean anything."

Juanita would not be dissuaded. "Yes, it does. It means I can be your flower girl. I'll save my basket."

"Hold up the bouquet," the wedding photographer told Mary, and she had to oblige, aware the pictures would show her as pink-faced and unsmiling. The photographer's flash temporarily blinded her, and when the picture taking finally ended, Mary handed the bouquet to Janet Brown.

"Would you put this in the kitchen cooler? Anita might want to preserve it later."

"I will—that's a good idea."

When Janet left, Mary turned to see a grinning Walter Chance at her side. "Good catch!"

She shrugged, aware Walter probably wouldn't believe she hadn't wanted the bridal bouquet. Many women in Rockdale probably thought Walter Chance was a good catch for some lucky woman, since he had money and his shrewish mother was no longer meddling in his life.

Mary fantasized about putting a notice in the *Record*, addressed to all single-but-searching women in Rockdale and surrounding Rock County: *Attention, ladies! Want a man willing to spend money on you? Contact Walter Chance at Chance*

Realty during normal business hours or leave him a voice-mail message.

Seeing Mary smile without knowing the cause, Walter apparently took new hope and squeezed her hand.

fifteen

Mary and her father had kept the same Sunday ritual for years. Both rose early and read favorite sections of the newspaper before going to First Church for Sunday school and morning worship. From there, they went to Rockdale Country Club's Sunday buffet. Lately, however—or, more specifically, since Evelyn Trent had become an important part of Judge Wayne Oliver's life, there had been fewer "normal" Sundays. Evelyn liked going other places to eat after church, often with her brother David and his family, and sometimes with Mary's father.

On this Sunday morning, Wayne Oliver told Mary he and Evelyn were planning to have lunch in Chattanooga.

"You'll miss the reception for Community's new associate pastor," Mary pointed out.

"I've already met him, and so has Evelyn. You can have our share of the little sandwiches and cakes and doodads."

"There will be plenty of those, I'm sure—Community does such things well."

"You can give Abbott my best wishes—I don't remember his first name."

"Jason. Jason Abbott."

"A pastor with a name from Greek mythology?"

"Jason is the Greek name for Joshua. It's in the Bible—a man named Jason was the Jewish convert who took Paul in at Thessalonica."

"You know more about the Bible than I do—I'll have to take your word that this particular Jason isn't a heathen."

Mary knew her father wasn't serious, but his remark made her realize she knew nothing about Jason Abbott's background, except that he and Ann Ward were cousins. Not, of course, that she should. *He's at Community Church, and I'm at First. We share an interest in our churches' children's programs, period.*

⁊⧫

As the eleven o'clock worship service began, Mary wished Jason Abbott could hear the grand swell of the pipe organ and see the sun stream through the stained glass windows. It would never happen, though. He would always worship at Community Church, and she at First. *And that was that.*

However, Mary went to Jason's reception. The number of cars in the parking lot suggested many of Rockdale's residents had turned out for the occasion.

On her way into the church, Mary saw Audra Hurley, a high school classmate married to Police Chief Earl Hurley, the son of Community's pastor.

"I can't wait for you to meet our new associate pastor," Audra gushed. "You'll just *love* him."

"We've met," Mary said.

"Oh, that's right, Earl mentioned Jason filled in for his dad at the rehearsal. Wasn't that the most touching wedding? I cried so much I went through three tissues."

"It was a lovely ceremony," Mary agreed.

"I'll see you later—I'm a hostess."

A little of Audra goes a long way. In their high school days, Audra Benson had led the in crowd of girls who delighted in making Mary miserable. It hadn't been easy, but with the Lord's help, Mary had forgiven Audra and the others for the pain they'd caused her, often thoughtlessly. While Mary and Audra could never be close friends like she and Toni were, they'd worked together well on several community projects, including their high school class tenth reunion.

When Mary entered the fellowship hall, Toni Trent greeted her. "I'm glad you came. I don't have to ask why your father isn't with you—I know he and Evelyn went somewhere after church."

"Chattanooga, I think. Anyway, he's already met Jason."

"So have you, but go through the reception line, anyway. I want Pastor Hurley to see all the non-Community people."

While she waited in line, Mary noticed Jason Abbott wore a dark gray suit that looked new but didn't quite fit. His conservatively patterned tie was a good choice, but he kept running his finger under the neck of his shirt, the way Mary's father did when his collars had too much starch. *Jason Abbott needs someone to oversee his wardrobe.*

Mary quickly dismissed the thought. He reputedly had found such a person, and in any case, the way he dressed was none of her business.

But where was his fiancée? Mary had presumed she would be at the reception, but apparently she hadn't come. Jason stood between Pastor and Mrs. Hurley to greet those who had come to meet him.

Mary noticed Jason looked into each person's eyes as if genuinely interested in knowing more about them, just as he had done with her. The people's smiles made it clear the new associate pastor was winning many friends.

When it was Mary's turn to be introduced, Jason told Mrs. Hurley they'd already met. "Mary shared some wonderful information about First's children's programs with me."

"Good," said Pastor Hurley. "I hope you'll continue to help us out. As I told Jason, seeing to the children will be his top priority."

Mary believed she'd already given Jason Abbott all the information he needed, but to be polite, she nodded. "Of course. If there's anything else I can do, please let me know."

Jason smiled. "As a matter of fact, I have several things to discuss with you."

He turned to meet the couple behind her, and Mary went to the refreshment table, which looked suspiciously like the one from which she'd served punch the day before.

"Recognize the tablecloth?" asked Toni. "Janet and I recycled it from the wedding reception. We put a sandwich tray over the stain where someone spilled punch."

"That was one of Hawk's twin teenaged cousins. Tom or Tim—I never could tell them apart," Mary said.

"You did a good job yesterday," Toni said. "In fact, things couldn't have gone better."

Audra Hurley came over to survey the refreshment table. "Hi, Toni and Mary. I'm supposed to tell the kitchen hostesses if we're low on anything."

"The cucumber sandwich tray needs refilling, but everything else looks all right," Toni said. "I'd say things are going well."

Audra snickered. "The refreshments are, anyway. See Mother Hurley's corsage? We ordered it for Jason's fiancée. We thought she'd be here today."

"Why isn't she?" asked Toni.

Audra shrugged. "I don't know. Pastor Hurley said no one was coming, period. No reason."

"She's missing a good chance to meet everyone," Toni said.

Mary wanted to hear more about Jason Abbott's phantom fiancée, but someone else spoke to Toni, and Audra returned to the kitchen.

"This is an excellent turnout," Janet said.

"Yes, it is." Mary glanced at the receiving line, where Jason Abbott continued talking to all comers. "He must be getting thirsty. Someone should give him something to drink."

"The punch is too sweet. I'll get him a glass of water. Thanks for the suggestion—I'm sure he'll appreciate it."

When Janet handed Jason the glass, she pointed to Mary. He mouthed "thanks" as he lifted the glass in a mock toast, and Mary returned his smile.

Toni noticed the exchange between them. "What was that all about?"

"Nothing. I thought Jason needed something to drink, and Janet apparently told him so."

"Jason Abbott's a really nice person—I can't imagine what would keep his fiancée from being here today."

Neither can I. "I should be going," Mary said.

"I'll see you at the meeting," Toni said.

For a moment, Mary's mind went blank, and she almost asked "What meeting?" before she remembered. "Yes. I hope the Civic Improvement Association on Tuesday night will have as good a turnout as this reception."

"Maybe you should have announced Jason would be on the program," Toni said lightly. "He'd be quite a draw."

"Yes, since Rockdale folks are so curious about anyone new. Too bad we didn't think of it before."

Toni laughed. "I'll tell him you said so. Good-bye, Mary."

&

Mary had just changed into more comfortable clothes and settled down to finish the Sunday paper when the telephone rang.

"Mary? I'm glad I caught you at home. Are you busy this afternoon?"

She recognized Todd Walker's distinctive radio-announcer voice immediately. "I have been—I just got home. Are you in Rockdale?"

"Next thing to it—I'm staying at DeSoto State Park. I'd like to come by if you'll be home this afternoon."

"I will, but my father isn't here."

"No matter—you're the one I want to see."

"I'll be here," Mary said.

"Good. I'm on my way."

Why would a handsome man like Todd Walker waste a beautiful summer afternoon on me?

"It can't be anything personal," Mary said aloud, but the sudden rapid beating of her heart betrayed her.

Mary had a matter of minutes to make herself presentable before Todd Walker arrived. She put on calf-length white cotton pants and topped them with a long red-and-white striped short-sleeved blouse. With the addition of red-and-white earrings shaped like anchors, her ensemble was complete.

"Not bad," Mary told the hall mirror, then shook her head at her vanity. She had learned to make the most of her positive attributes so her size wouldn't be the first thing anyone might notice about her. Yet Mary never expected to attract the kind of attention from men that other women could almost take for granted.

She turned from the mirror as the doorbell rang.

"You must have broken the speed limit to get here so quickly," she told Todd.

"I cheated. I was on my way when I called you on my cell phone."

Mary motioned Todd to come inside. He pointed to his white twill slacks and red-and-white plaid shirt, then to her outfit.

"Looks like we had the same idea about a color scheme today," he said.

"You already know how much I like red."

"You should—it's your color, no doubt about it."

The compliment embarrassed Mary, and she spoke quickly. "Thanks. Can I get you something to drink?"

"No, thanks. We'll have something later, if you like. Right now, we're going for a ride."

"Will hiking be required?"

"Not this time. I'm in the convertible again, though, so you'll want a hat."

Mary took a wide-brimmed white straw hat from the hall closet. "I'm ready," she announced.

"You look very fetching, Miss Oliver. Your carriage awaits."

When they started to his car, Mary glanced across the street and Todd smiled. "I don't see your neighbor. Too bad— I would have invited her to come with us."

Mary laughed and took her place in the front passenger seat. Todd started the engine and turned the car around in the street. "Have you made progress on the bluff property we looked at last week?"

"Yes. I hope to close the deal tomorrow, but I decided to come a day sooner."

"Any particular reason?"

Todd glanced at her. "I wanted to see you."

Mary opened her mouth, then closed it quickly when her

mind didn't immediately provide her with anything intelligent to say.

Todd appeared to be leaving town, but on the other side of the bridge, he pulled into a pocket-sized roadside park and stopped.

"I subscribe to the Rockdale newspaper now. When my copy came on Saturday, I read a story about a meeting of the Rockdale Civic Improvement Association Tuesday night."

Thinking Todd hadn't meant anything personal by saying he wanted to see her, Mary felt herself relax. "I know—I wrote it."

Todd didn't seem surprised. "It's a good article, but I wonder how many of the people in the organization really want to improve the community."

"All of them, of course. That's the whole idea."

"Yes, but exactly what is their idea of improvement? We're going back into town and drive around. When we do, I want you to try to forget you live here."

"Why?"

"Because until you see a place as an outsider, it's hard to detect any need for improvement."

"Oh, I think many of us know Rockdale could be a better place to live. The only question is how to accomplish it."

"Go along with me on this, Mary. Close your eyes, and when you open them on my count of ten, you will be seeing Rockdale for the first time. Understand?"

"I suppose so." Mary sighed, then closed her eyes. As Todd began his countdown, she stifled an impulse to laugh. *Your eyes are getting heavy—you will hear only my voice and you will do what I say. . . .*

Mary had never been hypnotized, but she thought Todd's smooth voice was well suited for such a practice.

"Three—two—one. Open your eyes. You are now prepared to see Rockdale in an entirely new way."

Mary had no idea what to expect, but she was willing to try to do as he directed. As Todd drove slowly through town, he asked her what she saw.

"A beautiful old courthouse," Mary said when they reached the square.

"Now what?" asked Todd when they reached Rockdale Boulevard.

"I hadn't really noticed it before, but a few businesses along here do look a little shabby."

"How long has that building been for sale?" he asked when they passed a neglected storefront.

"I don't know—a few months. Daniel Smith's copy shop was there, and after he left town no one wanted to take it over."

"Does Rockdale have any upscale restaurants?" he asked.

"No."

"How about grocery stores? Are they clean and well stocked and large enough?"

"I don't have any trouble finding what I need," Mary said somewhat defensively.

"Remember, you're supposed to see the stores as an outsider, maybe someone from a place with lots of different kinds of chain stores. Do you find them here?"

"No, but I like to shop with people I know personally. You don't have that advantage in a bigger place."

Todd shook his head. "You're not playing by the rules." He reached the end of Rockdale Boulevard and pointed to the mountain rising before them. "One of Rockdale's biggest problems is staring you in the face right now."

"Rockdale Ridge? What's wrong with it?"

"Do you know who owns it?"

Mary shrugged. "Some lumber company, I think. Maybe the state has part of it. Why?"

"There's a major highway not three miles on the other side of that ridge. If Rockdale Boulevard were to be extended to meet it, the town would boom."

"Not everyone wants Rockdale to grow," Mary said.

"Unfortunately, that's a problem. The city fathers should be thinking about the benefits of planned growth. It could transform this whole area."

Mary didn't understand Todd's enthusiasm. "What's your interest in all of this?"

"My roots are here. I want Rockdale to be the best place it can be."

"What do you propose to do about it?"

He put the car in reverse and turned it around. "We can talk about that over dinner."

"Not much is open around here on Sunday night."

Todd grinned. "My point exactly. We're going elsewhere."

sixteen

This time when Todd took the road out of town and kept going, Mary thought he might be going to Mentone again. Instead, he turned onto the road leading to DeSoto State Park.

"I'm surprised you're staying at DeSoto Lodge," she said.

"It's usually full this time of the year, but I got a cancellation. Since it's halfway between Rockdale and Mentone, it's an ideal location. The food's good, and I thought you might enjoy dining there tonight."

Again, Mary thought. "I will, thank you. You haven't said how long you plan to stay."

"As long as it takes to do what's needed." Todd pulled into the lodge's parking lot and shut off the engine. "You have a subtle way of asking questions."

Mary returned his smile. "That's what teachers do."

"Relax. This is summertime. You're not on duty now."

Todd opened the car door and took Mary's hand. "The dining room hasn't opened yet, so we have time to visit the falls."

Mary pointed to her shoes, the same open-toed sandals she'd worn when Todd took her to Mentone. "You said we wouldn't be hiking."

"We're not. You've been here often enough to know the path to the falls is more a walk than a hike. In fact, I checked it out earlier today, and I can certify it's sandal safe."

"In that case, I suppose I'll go. It's been a long time since I've seen the falls."

As he had done in Mentone, Todd held Mary's hand as they walked. The afternoon was warm without being oppressively hot. Neither spoke, and Mary sensed Todd was enjoying the beauty of God's creation as much as she was, and like her, hesitated to spoil it by speaking.

They reached the top of the path, where water cascaded over a series of small waterfalls. Todd continued to hold Mary's hand even after they were seated on a bench overlooking the foaming stream.

For a time, the only sounds were those made by the falling water and calling birds. Finally, Todd broke their long silence. "Do you know you're very good company?"

Mary shook her head. "I don't know why you'd say that."

"Because it's true. Many otherwise attractive females talk too much. I can't stand a chatterbox. You're not like that. When you talk, you have something to say. I like that."

As if to prove him right, Mary said nothing, unable to think of anything sensible. She thought of the blond she'd met in Mentone and wondered if Todd considered Veronica, his fellow Haskell Holdings employee, a chatterbox.

"I've told you something I like about you," Todd said after a moment. "You're free to return the favor."

Mary smiled faintly. She'd never tell Todd Walker he'd been the love of her young life, so she said the first thing which came into her mind. "I suppose you know you have a wonderful voice. I like to listen to it, even when I don't understand what you say."

Todd laughed. "You've obviously never heard me sing. As for what I say, I know I tend to get carried away at times. What I've been trying to tell you all afternoon is simple. I'd hate to see the town of Rockdale dry up and die because a handful of its people are afraid of progress."

Mary quickly defended Rockdale's leaders. "It's not that way at all—the Civic Improvement Association wants to manage change, not stop it."

"It remains to be seen how they'll go about doing that."

"What do you think they should do?"

Todd smiled wryly. "Lots of things. For one thing, Rockdale needs more than one road to the outside world. For another, Rockdale and all of Rock County need to capitalize on their natural resources. Except for a little logging here and there, the land's going to waste."

Mary didn't know enough about those subjects to agree or disagree with Todd. "Come to the meeting Tuesday night and say so. They really want people to speak their minds."

"I intend to be there as an observer. I haven't lived in Rockdale for years, and I wouldn't want it to seem like I'm sticking my nose where it doesn't belong."

"If you care enough to take time off from work to come to the meeting, you deserve to be heard."

Todd looked away. "I'm not exactly taking time off from work."

He looks almost guilty. "I don't understand. What does Haskell Holdings have to do with Rockdale?"

Todd looked back at Mary. "Nothing. I'm here to check out some things in the area, that's all."

The thought occurred to Mary that Haskell Holdings could be one of the nameless entities rumored to want to buy land around Rockdale. If so, had Todd come to Rockdale on his behalf—or theirs?

Before Mary could find a tactful way to ask him about it, Todd glanced at his watch and stood. "The dining room should be open now. I haven't eaten since breakfast, and I make it a policy never to say anything important on an empty stomach."

Mary realized he was teasing and smiled. "And I make it a policy never to say anything important to a man at any time."

Todd's finger sketched an imaginary line in the air. "Bravo! Chalk one up for Miss Mary Oliver. She may not say much, but when she does, watch out!"

Todd held her hand all the way back to the lodge. At the porch, he stopped. "I want to get something from my cabin. I'll be back in a minute. Wait in the lobby—the mosquitoes will be thick on the porch this time of day."

Mary went to the ladies' room and ran a comb through her hair and powdered her nose. The mirror reflected unnaturally bright eyes, and her cheeks glowed, partly with the remnants of the sunburn she'd gotten the last time she was with Todd. The other cause, she suspected, also had something to do with him.

When Mary came back into the lobby, the dining room hostess spoke to her. *Sally Richmond, now Morgan,* she remembered.

"Hello, Mary. Are you and Walter here again this evening?"

"Hi, Sally. I am, he isn't."

"You're alone, then?"

Todd arrived in time to hear their exchange. "No, Sally. The lady's with me."

Sally looked flustered, and Mary remembered she and Todd had attended Rockdale High at the same time. From the way Sally and Todd looked at each other, she guessed they had dated.

"Good. As you can see, we're not at all crowded tonight. You can sit where you like."

Todd pointed to a window overlooking the lawn, now deeply shadowed. "Over there will be fine."

Sally led them to the table where Mary had sat when she met Jason Abbott for the first time, not a week ago.

"Do you come here often?" Todd asked.

"Not really, but in the past week I've been here for both lunch and dinner."

"Then maybe you can tell me what to order."

"I don't know what you like."

Todd smiled faintly. "I hope you're beginning to."

When the waitress came to the table, Todd waved off the menu and ordered two catfish dinners.

"I presume you love fried catfish and hush puppies as much now as you did when you were a kid."

"When did you ever see me eat catfish?" she asked.

"At a family reunion at my grandmother's house. The men had gone fishing that morning, and the women fried their catch. I was about ten, so you must have been all of five years old. I remember my mother telling your father you were eating too fast, and you might swallow a bone."

Mary didn't remember ever having catfish at Todd Walker's grandmother's house. "I think you made that up."

Todd smiled. "I guess that day didn't make as much of an impression on you as it did on me. Anyway, I brought these to show you." He opened the briefcase he had brought from his room and handed Mary a sheaf of detailed architect's drawings.

She read the heading of the first aloud. "Millican's Bluff: Concept One."

"What do you think of it?"

"It looks like a new building trying to pretend to be an old farmhouse."

Todd looked delighted. "That's exactly what I think. Check out the others and tell me which you like best."

Mary examined the drawings, which she took to be increasingly elaborate treatments of someone's idea of what should be built on Millican's Bluff, ranging from a restaurant to a medium-sized hotel and a large resort. Then she handed them back to Todd without comment.

"Well?" he prompted. "If you were in charge, which would you choose to build?"

"None of them. I would leave that gorgeous view alone."

Todd looked disappointed. "You know that's not going to happen. The land's just going to waste now. Think of all the money this project will pump into the area—all the people it will put to work."

"I know—but I still don't like spoiling God's natural beauty with artificial things, and I wouldn't want anything like that for Rockdale, either."

Todd drew back as if she had slapped him. "There's no danger of that. But towns are like people. They move forward, or they wither and die."

Which am I, Todd, withering or moving ahead? "Since you feel so strongly about it, come to the meeting Tuesday night and say so." *And stop badgering me about it,* Mary's expression added.

Todd's sudden smile surprised Mary. "I like your style, Mary. You're not afraid to speak your mind."

"Thanks," she said dryly. Todd's compliment wasn't exactly the kind to flutter a female heart. But then, Mary acknowledged, for years Todd Walker had that effect on her without saying a word or doing anything—something he would never know.

"Two catfish dinners," the waitress said. "Careful, the plates are hot."

"I really missed this kind of food in California."

"They don't have catfish? No wonder you came back."

By the time they finished eating, the sun had gone down and the sky had deepened into a purple twilight. On the drive back to Rockdale, Mary raised her face to the cool evening air and let it blow through her hair. Todd put on a CD of big band era instrumentals, and Mary leaned back into the soft leather upholstery and closed her eyes, relaxing as the music and the wind swirled around her.

The next thing she knew, Todd was shaking her shoulder. "Wake up—you're home."

Mary opened her eyes and sat up. "I wasn't asleep," she protested, but she hadn't remembered crossing the bridge back into town.

Todd came around and opened the door. "Looks like I'm too late for the garden tour," he said when they started down the walk.

"I'm afraid it's too dark to see anything now, but you can probably smell the jasmine and honeysuckle."

"Oh, yes—no man-made perfume can beat the real thing."

In the near-darkness, Mary fumbled with her key, unable to see the front door lock.

"Let me do that." Todd's hand brushed hers, and when the door swung open, he put his arms around Mary.

"So soft," he murmured.

Surprised by his sudden move, Mary stood quietly and waited to see what would happen next.

When he tightened his embrace, Mary instinctively raised her face to accept a kiss which seemed to last a long time.

When Todd released her, Mary realized they were standing in the doorway, half in and half out of the house. "We should close the door."

Todd stepped into the dark hall, pushed the door shut with his foot, and kissed Mary again.

Leaving one arm around his neck, Mary reached for the light switch with the other. When the light came on, Todd jumped back, startled. "Who turned on that light?"

"I did."

Todd looked sheepish. "I thought maybe the judge was lying in wait with his shotgun. I'd better leave before he gets home."

Mary smiled. "I've never known my father to point a shotgun at anyone."

"I don't want to be the first." Todd started for the door, then stopped to kiss Mary again, this time quite briefly. "I'll call you," he said, and with a final wave he was gone.

Before Mary closed the door behind Todd, she saw Sally Proffitt on her porch swing, outlined in the faint glow of her living room windows. Mary sighed and went back into the house, aware of two things—a man she had once adored had just kissed her, and if, as she suspected, Sally Proffitt had seen it, everyone in Rockdale would soon know it.

seventeen

Mary had just gotten out of bed Monday morning when she heard the back door close, signaling her father's departure. When she went into the kitchen for breakfast, Mary found his note on the small corkboard by the calendar.

You were in bed when I got home and still asleep when I left. If you have time today, my tan suit needs to go to the cleaners.

The note was typical of those they had exchanged over the years, brief and to the point. It said nothing about his and Evelyn's trip to Chattanooga or what time he'd gotten home. Of course, her father didn't know everything about Mary's time with Todd, either.

Mary glanced at the calendar for the week ahead. Except for an appointment for a haircut Tuesday morning and the Rockdale Civic Improvement Association meeting that night, the squares were blessedly blank.

"I can use some time off," she said aloud. Mary had books to read and letters to write, but her first priority for the day was the garden.

After breakfast she put on the jeans, oversized shirt, and straw hat she'd worn on Decoration Day and started weeding the front flower bed and cutting the woody stems of bloomed-out hostas. As she worked, Mary thought about Todd Walker. She suspected the interest he'd shown in the Olivers' garden was more feigned than genuine.

Like his sudden interest in me. Mary couldn't believe that a handsome man like Todd Walker, up and coming in the business world, had twice sought her out, taken her to lunch and dinner—and then kissed her. Mary reviewed every word he'd spoken the night before. *You're good company,* he'd said.

Mary sighed. *So is a golden retriever.* Although Todd had

seemed to want to kiss her, she knew she shouldn't entertain romantic notions about him. If, as she vaguely suspected, Todd Walker had some hidden reason for paying her attention, she would be neither surprised nor hurt.

Mary worked in the flower beds for two hours, went inside for water and a brief rest, then spent another thirty minutes on the small plot by the kitchen door where her father had put out a dozen tomato and red and green pepper plants. He called it "his" garden, but Mary usually wound up weeding and mulching it. Noting the tomato plants would soon need staking, she posted a reminder to that effect on the cork bulletin board.

Mary was in the shower when the telephone rang. *Todd Walker* was her first thought—he'd promised to call. Then she decided it probably wasn't Todd, since he had business to transact that day and wouldn't likely be free to call until evening, if at all.

Mary towel-dried her hair and dressed in slacks and a knit top before going to the answering machine. She hadn't noticed it when she came inside, but the display showed two messages.

The first was from Walter Chance. "Hi, Mary. I'm making reservations at Mentone for Thursday night, so go ahead and mark your calendar. I'll catch you at the meeting tomorrow night—I'll be pretty much tied up until then. Have a great day!"

Mary could picture Walter smiling eagerly as he recorded the message. She felt irritated he took it for granted she would go out with him, but almost everything Walter Chance did these days seemed to grate on her nerves.

Where is your Christian attitude? Mary's conscience asked. *You should be thinking kind thoughts toward this man who thinks so much of you.*

I can't be too nice. Given an inch, Walter will take a mile.

Mary's conscience eventually won every argument, and this was no exception. *All right, I'll be kind to Walter, but that doesn't mean I have to go to dinner with him Thursday—or any other time.*

Having settled her mind about that, Mary played the second message, which was from another familiar and more welcome voice. "This is Jason Abbott calling for Mary Oliver. Thanks for coming to the reception yesterday. When you have a minute, please call me."

He added the church phone number and his extension, which Mary wrote down and dialed immediately. She feared she'd get his voice mail, but after the phone rang a few times, Jason answered, sounding a bit out of breath.

"Did I catch you at a bad time?"

"I was on my way to see Pastor Hurley when I heard my office telephone ring. I didn't know I could still sprint so fast. Thanks for returning my call. I thought you might be taking a well-deserved vacation this week."

"I was gardening this morning."

"I don't want to impose on you, since you've already given me so much help, but our church leaders are planning to remodel the educational wing. They hope you'll give us some good ideas."

"I don't know anything about remodeling a church," Mary said.

"You don't have to. It'll be some time before we add to the present space, but in the meantime, could you look at what we have now and give us some suggestions for improvement?"

Mary visualized Jason bent over the telephone, speaking earnestly, perhaps running his free hand through his unruly brown hair, and knew she couldn't refuse. "I don't know what sort of help I'd be—I know Community has an excellent Bible study program."

"That's true, but the children's space needs immediate improvement. You can help us with that if you can spare the time."

Mary pictured her almost-blank calendar. "I'm free on Wednesday. I can come by Community that morning, if that's convenient."

"That'll be perfect—say about ten o'clock?"

"All right. And while I'm thinking about it, I hope you're coming to the Civic Improvement Association meeting at the high school tomorrow night."

"I don't know much about it, but Pastor Hurley mentioned I should go."

"Definitely. Rockdale is going to change, no matter what, and my father and some others think we need to decide what kind of changes we want and how we want them made."

"Sounds like a good idea. I hope to see you there Tuesday night—and at Community on Wednesday morning?"

"Yes. I'll be there at ten." Mary hung up the telephone and added "Community Church—10:00" to the previously blank calendar square for Wednesday. Mary didn't regard helping Jason Abbott as a chore. She was quite willing to share her knowledge with someone whose enthusiasm for helping children develop a relationship with their Creator seemed to match hers.

You wish he weren't already taken.

The idea came as clearly as if a voice had whispered it in her ear. As much as Mary would like to dismiss it, deep down, she admitted its truth.

❧

Mary's father called around noon on Monday to say the Rockdale CIA committee would meet that evening at their house. "I hope you don't mind, but I invited Walter to sit in with us if he's free."

"Thanks for the warning," Mary said. "What time?"

"Six-thirty. Should I pick up something on the way home?"

"Did you promise to feed them?"

"I mentioned we might have a few sandwiches and your famous orange mint iced tea."

"I have all the makings for that, but I wasn't planning on having company tonight."

"You're not—the committee is hardly company and they won't expect a feast."

"I'll take care of it."

"Thanks, puddin'. I can always count on you."

Mary smiled at his use of her pet name as she hung up the telephone. Over the years, her father had often called at the last minute to say he'd invited someone to supper. She enjoyed cooking and liked to prepare special dishes for guests.

She wasn't eager to see Walter Chance, but if he asked again, she'd tell him she wasn't going to Mentone with him on Thursday—or any other time.

But kindly, her conscience reminded her.

ᴥ

"Time to get started," Wayne Oliver announced shortly after six-thirty.

"Where's Walter?" asked Mayor Hastings. "I wanted to hear what he had to say about the quarry."

"He had to go out of town, according to Ellie Fergus, but she says he'll be back for the meeting tomorrow night."

Mary felt momentary relief, even thought Walter's absence only postponed the inevitable. "There are sandwiches on the dining room table and the tea's on the sideboard. Please help yourselves."

The committee members did so, then sat down to discuss about how the meeting should be conducted.

"We should have a good turnout," Sam Roberts said. "Everyone who's come into the store since the notice came out on Friday wanted to talk about it."

"I hear Rockdale folks might not be the only ones there," Margaret Hastings said.

"Who else is coming?" asked Dr. Endicott.

The mayor shrugged. "According to the grapevine, several big developers want to see what we're up to."

Mary immediately thought of Todd Walker, but she remained silent. She hadn't had a chance to talk to her father about Todd, and this was hardly the time to bring it up.

"I wish they would," Sam said. "I'd like to see them keep a straight face while they try to say big box stores won't ruin a dozen businesses like mine."

"Or that what they want to do to make money won't hurt the environment," said Newman Howell.

"We don't yet know that's the case," Wayne Oliver reminded them. "However, once we have tougher zoning laws, the big bullies will leave us alone."

"I'm all for that," said the doctor.

"We'll put zoning first on the agenda. What next?"

Mary dutifully took notes, but as talk about the next night's program swirled around her, she realized all three of the men who had recently shown some kind of interest in her would be at the meeting.

Walter, Todd, Jason—each man different, each with so much to offer.

"If Rockdale doesn't make good choices now, we might never have another chance," banker Newman Howell said as everyone stood to leave.

"I like that—we should use it as our slogan," the mayor said.

Maybe I should, too.

In her heart, Mary felt the community wasn't the only thing about to have to make hard choices.

⚭

As the committee hoped, many people turned out for the open meeting of the Rockdale Civic Improvement Association. Mary had lettered a banner inviting them to join the RCIA for a five-dollar donation, and she and Ellie Fergus sat at a table set up outside the auditorium doors. Mary took the money and Ellie added the names and addresses to the roster.

Among the first to arrive, Evelyn Trent had already made out her check. "I've heard so much about this meeting, I feel as if I'm on the committee myself. If your father talks about it as much at home as he does when we're together, you're probably tired of hearing about this association."

Mary smiled at Evelyn's resigned tone. "After tonight, I suspect he'll have time for other important things."

"Let's hope you're right."

"I always wondered what it would be like to belong to the

CIA," a man said.

Mary recognized his voice even before she looked up and saw his warm smile. "Hello, Jason. I'm glad you could come."

"You've cut your hair—I like it," he said.

Surprised he noticed, Mary murmured her thanks. Jason signed the list and had scarcely gone inside before Todd Walker appeared. He bent close to speak to Mary as if he didn't want to be overheard. "The bluff deal is a 'go,' but it's run me ragged the past two days. I wanted to call you last night, but some of the bigwigs came up from Birmingham to celebrate, and I couldn't get away."

Mary hadn't forgotten Todd's promise to call, but she didn't want him to think she felt disappointed he hadn't. "I'm glad things worked out for you."

"We can have our own celebration before I go back to Birmingham," Todd said. "How about lunch tomorrow?"

Mary thought of her commitment to Jason Abbott and shook her head. "Sorry, I'm tied up all day."

Todd looked disappointed. "In that case, I won't stay around tomorrow." He looked at her more closely and smiled. "Hey, I like your hair. There's even less to blow in the wind now."

Mary said nothing, but after Todd signed the list and moved on, Ellie Fergus shook her head. "It looks like my boss has some serious competition. Men don't usually notice a woman's hair has been cut, much less compliment her on it."

Mary chose her words carefully. "Todd Walker is one of my Austin cousins."

"And also one of the best football players Rockdale High ever sent to the university. I see Todd has a Birmingham address—what's he doing in Rockdale?"

That's a good question. "His roots are here."

"Maybe his job is, too—I hear he works for Haskell Holdings."

"Yes. They just bought property around Mentone."

"Walter tried to get that land himself."

Maybe that's where he went yesterday. "I didn't know that.

Where is Walter? I haven't seen him tonight."

"He came early to set up the sound system. I'm sure he'll find you before the night is over."

Unfortunately.

Mary was relieved when others arrived at the membership table, ending their conversation. She didn't like to discuss either Todd Walker or Walter Chance with Ellie, or anyone else.

When they heard Judge Oliver calling the meeting to order, Ellie urged Mary to go inside. "Don't you need to write minutes or something? I'll stay out here for the latecomers."

"All the comments will be recorded, so I won't take notes. I doubt if any one person could possibly keep up with everything, anyway."

Ellie smiled. "Or with all your admirers?"

Instead of denying she had admirers, Mary answered lightly. "They're under control, at least for now. Chief Hurley and Deputy Henson are both here in case a fight breaks out."

Ellie's laughter followed Mary into the auditorium, where Mayor Hastings invited the crowd to stand for the Pledge of Allegiance.

Mary thought the committee had chosen an excellent way to begin the meeting. What it would accomplish and how it would end remained to be seen.

eighteen

The auditorium was crowded, and after each of the original Rockdale CIA members made their opening statements, half the audience seemed to want a turn at the microphone. Mary stood at the rear of the auditorium and listened. When Todd Walker came forward to speak, a ripple of conversation swept through the crowd as people recognized then applauded him.

"Thanks, friends," he said when the applause died down. "It's nice to know my home town hasn't forgotten me. I haven't forgotten y'all, either, and that's why I'm here tonight."

Each speaker was limited to three minutes, but Todd talked much longer. Mary didn't know when or how he'd learned public speaking, but he obviously knew how to use his powerful voice.

"A town like Rockdale will grow or die. The right outside interests will bring jobs and offer advantages you'd never have otherwise. Don't make the mistake of trying to keep everyone out, just because you're afraid things will change. They're going to do that anyway. It's up to all of us to make sure the changes are good ones."

When Todd Walker finished speaking to restrained applause, Walter Chance took the microphone.

"What Mr. Walker says is true up to a point, folks. The thing is, he doesn't live here now, and we do. Rockdale is ours, and if we don't take steps to protect it from the wrong kind of change, it'll be too late to complain about what happens. In case you don't know it, our zoning laws are a mess. It won't do much good to talk about pie-in-the-sky progress when we're mired down in mud-pie zoning."

The crowd laughed and applauded Walter. He lacked Todd Walker's ease or grace, but he'd obviously impressed the audience.

Who would have suspected it? Now that he was on his own, Walter Chance seemed on his way to becoming a community leader.

Other speakers followed. Most were complimentary of the CIA, but a few called them "the same old crowd."

"They're trying to fleece the city while crying wolf, but we won't let them pull the wool over our eyes!" one man declared, miffed when his mixed metaphor drew unintended laughter.

When it was obvious every relevant point had been made, Wayne Oliver stood and asked those present to help those in authority make needed changes. "If you haven't already signed up with the Civic Improvement Association, stop by the table on your way out and put your money where your mouth is. If you're willing to help on any of the committees we've talked about tonight, we have sign-up sheets for that, too."

"We do?" Mary asked Ellie, who had joined her to hear the final speakers.

"I think your father made that up on the spot, but I brought several spare legal pads."

"We'd better get busy and put them out."

After calling another meeting in two weeks, Wayne Oliver adjourned the first Rockdale Civic Improvement Association general gathering. Enough people came to the membership table to keep Ellie and Mary busy for another half hour. Mary expected Todd Walker to stop by, but apparently he had already left.

Wayne Oliver came out of the auditorium as Mary and Ellie were tallying the evening's contributions. "We can count the money later. It's been a long day, and I'm tired."

"Go on, Judge. I'll take Mary home."

Mary didn't see Walter until he spoke. Remembering her promise to her conscience to be nice to him, Mary forced a smile. "You don't have to do that, Walter. I'm ready to leave. By the way, you did a good job tonight. I didn't know you were such an accomplished speaker."

Walter glowed. "You think so? Maybe I should have left out the mud-pie part."

"Not at all—it made your point well," Mary's father said. "Come on, Mary. Ellie and Walter can deposit the money in the RCIA account tomorrow, can't you?"

"Of course," Ellie said. "I'll make a copy of the deposit slip for you."

Undaunted, Walter grinned. "I'll even deliver it to Mary in person."

Good. I won't be at home.

"That won't be necessary," Wayne Oliver said. "Drop it off at the courthouse."

"I'll see you later," Walter added to Mary.

"Walter did well tonight," her father said on the way to his car. "It's too bad you don't return his feelings, but from what I hear, he's not the only fish on your string."

"What are you talking about?"

"Todd Walker. Apparently several people saw you with him Sunday."

Sally Proffitt strikes again. "It's not secret—as I told you, he dropped in unexpectedly. You could have gone to dinner with us if you'd been here."

"I don't think either of you would have liked that."

"Todd's my cousin," she reminded him.

"Kissing cousin, apparently. After his speech tonight, I'm convinced Todd's company has some kind of plans for Rockdale. I wish I knew what he was up to."

"Then ask him."

"The next time he comes to see you, I will." Wayne Oliver rubbed his shoulder. "This was quite an interesting night. I think change is definitely in the air."

"So it is," Mary agreed, but she doubted she and her father were thinking about the same things.

⁂

Mary reached Community Church at precisely three minutes before ten on Wednesday morning and saw Jason Abbott waiting for her just inside the main entrance. Mary recognized the shirt and slacks he'd worn the day they met; neither seemed to have been pressed since.

Jason smiled and extended his hand. "Thanks for coming. I see you brought a clipboard."

"I like to take notes and make sketches when I tour a facility, and my clipboard serves the purpose well."

"Another good idea. Would you like coffee or a sweet roll before we start? Mrs. Hurley keeps us well supplied."

"No, thank you. I'm ready to begin the tour."

"Follow me, then."

Mary quickly understood why Community wanted to add more space. The church had grown tremendously in the last few years, and rooms which had once been adequate for infants, toddlers, and other preschool groups were now crowded. Children's classes had been moved into larger rooms recently vacated by older youth and adults, who now met in portables outside the church proper. However, nothing had been done to make the children's new spaces attractive.

As Jason had done at First, Mary asked a few questions and made notes as they went. "These halls would be perfect for Bible school murals."

"I don't know if our youth are as talented as the ones who did yours," Jason said.

"No talent required—I can show you how to take a sketch and enlarge it on a grid projected on the wall. From there, it's a matter of coloring in the lines."

When Pastor Hurley saw them in the hall, he invited Mary and Jason into his office, where they talked for some time.

"Tell your father I think the Civic Improvement Association is off to a good start," the pastor said when Jason and Mary stood to leave.

"He's worked very hard on it. He'll be glad to hear that."

"I thought it was a productive meeting," Jason told Mary when they left Pastor Hurley's office. "Rockdale seems fine the way it is, but I suppose there's always room for improvement."

Mary glanced at her wristwatch, ready to make a graceful exit, but Jason didn't seem to want her to go.

"I'll show you my office. After I check my messages, we'll go to lunch."

"Oh, no, you don't have to do that."

"I want to."

Mary followed Jason down a narrow hall to a small office filled with boxes marked "books."

"Excuse the mess. I seem to have a larger library than Community has shelves."

"Cozy," Mary commented. The word sounded better than her first impression: cramped.

"It's adequate. When the educational facilities are remodeled, I'm told I'll have a much larger office."

Mary stood near the door and looked around the windowless cubicle while Jason accessed the voice mailbox on his telephone. His desk was all but covered with assorted papers and folders. A small artificial African violet plant and a framed picture of a curly-haired child on one corner were the desk's only decorations.

"No messages," a hollow electronic voice reported, and Jason replied to it in the same robotic tones. "Thank you. Have a nice day."

Mary laughed. "You imitate your machine very well."

"Why not? Machines are always imitating us."

Mary pointed to the picture on his desk. "Who's the adorable child?"

"My nephew, Mack. That was taken last year just before his long curls were cut."

What about your fiancée? Where is her picture? Before Mary could summon the courage to speak, Jason asked if Statum's would be all right for lunch. "I'd rather go to DeSoto Park, but there isn't enough time for that today."

"You don't have to feed me at all," Mary repeated.

"I know, but I have a few more questions to ask about the primary department. Call it a business lunch."

Mary smiled faintly. "In that case, it's all right."

ꙮ

Statum's Family Restaurant was filled with the usual assortment of workers from nearby businesses and offices. In addition to the seated diners, many others came in for takeout service.

When Mary and Jason entered, Tom Statum motioned them to a just-cleared booth at one of the large plate glass windows. "Hello, Pastor Jason, Mary. Have a seat. Rita will be with you in a second."

Several diners turned to greet Jason or Mary or both, their eyebrows raised in question. If Jason noticed, he made no comment, and Mary saw no reason to point it out to him. *Every pastor lives in a fishbowl,* Mary once heard. *So does every teacher,* she had thought at the time. In a small town, anyone in those fishbowls was bound to be a topic of conversation.

"You've no doubt eaten here many times. What's good?" Jason asked.

"The plate lunches are excellent, but I don't usually have that much for lunch."

"Neither do I—in fact, I sometimes forget to eat at all. Pastor Hurley said I should stock my office with fruit and crackers and instant soup so I won't waste away."

"I don't know where he thinks you'd put anything else in that office," Mary said.

When the waitress appeared to take their orders, Mary said she would have her usual. "I will, too, whatever that is," Jason added.

The waitress looked doubtful. "Most men want more than a fruit salad plate. Wouldn't you rather have fries and a cheeseburger?"

"No," he said firmly, "but make my fruit salad a club sandwich on whole wheat, light on the mayo."

"Can do." The waitress took the menus and departed.

"I suppose you and your father must know everyone in town," Jason commented when Mary introduced him to several people who stopped by the booth.

"In a place this size, that's not hard. You must have grown up in a big city."

"A few towns and several cities. My father was a minister, and we hardly ever stayed in any one place more than four or five years."

"So you're a PK? A preacher's kid who became a preacher, no less. Ann didn't tell me that."

Jason smiled. "She still can't believe I followed in my father's footsteps. So many people assume ministers' families are going to be rebellious, and a lot of them turn out to be."

"But surely you weren't ever that way yourself?"

Jason's smile faded. "Only with the Lord."

Before Jason could explain his meaning, Walter Chance entered the restaurant and made a beeline for Mary.

Mary's heart sank as Walter looked from her to Jason and held out his hand. "I don't believe we've met, but you're Justin Abbott, Community's new assistant pastor, right? I'm Walter Chance. Chance is the name, and real estate's my game."

"Jason," Mary corrected as the men shook hands. "It's Jason Abbott."

"Close," said Walter, then returned his attention to Mary. "Our Mentone reservation is for seven," he said clearly. "I'll pick you up around six."

Mary groaned inwardly, not only because of what Walter had said, but because Jason Abbott—and everyone else in the restaurant—had heard it.

"I can't go," she said, but Walter had already turned away to pick up his takeout order. It would only make matters worse if she followed him to repeat she wasn't going to Mentone.

"Nice fellow you have there," Jason said cautiously.

"He's not my fellow. I've been trying to tell him so for days, but he won't listen."

Did I actually tell Jason Abbott that? Mary closed her eyes and put her hands to her flaming cheeks in embarrassment.

She opened her eyes and saw Jason's amused look. "I don't

know why anyone wouldn't want to listen to you. I certainly enjoy it."

You do? Mary sipped her water and felt her composure gradually returning. *Thanks to Jason Abbott.* He had turned what could have been a humiliating experience into something positive.

"In fact," Jason continued, "I'd like it very much if you could show me some of the local sights tomorrow. I know you're a good tour guide."

"Tomorrow?"

"Yes. Consider it as a community service."

"In that case, I don't suppose I can refuse."

"Good. I have a couple of early appointments, but I should be free around ten. We can have lunch at DeSoto State Park after the city tour."

"Here's your order."

Until Rita set the platters on the table between them, Mary hadn't realized she'd been leaning forward, hanging on Jason's every word. Once more she felt everyone in the restaurant must have noticed.

"Is tomorrow settled, then?" Jason asked when Rita left.

"Yes. I look forward to it."

Mary meant every word.

nineteen

For her role as Jason Abbott's tour leader, Mary settled on a lime green pantsuit with a long, slimming top. She further prepared by wearing walking shoes, locating her straw hat, and putting bug spray in her purse.

Just before ten o'clock, Mary looked out and saw Sally Proffitt sweeping her front walk. A moment later, Jason's car stopped in front of Mary's house. She watched him get out of the car and wave to her neighbor and opened the front door in time to hear their shouted agreement it was a lovely morning.

"It seems you've made a new friend," Mary commented when they started down the walk.

"I hope so. Being new in town, I need all of those I can get."

Mary waved to Sally Proffitt while Jason opened the car door for her. Friend or not, Sally probably wondered what Jason and Mary were up to now.

"Where would you like to start your tour?" Mary asked.

"Pastor Hurley took me around the main streets and showed me the park, but I haven't seen the town from the ridges. Even though Community Church is right at Warren Mountain, I've never been to the top."

"We'll go there first."

"I talked to Ann last night," Jason said on the way. "She was happy to hear we'd met and said to tell you she's glad you're helping me."

"She'll be a wonderful teacher. I hope we can stay in touch."

"Ann feels the same way."

At the summit, Mary directed Jason to the grassy area used as a parking lot for the amphitheater built into the far side of the mountain. "Community has a beautiful Easter Sunrise service here every year. My father and I never miss it."

Jason was obviously impressed. "I can see why. This is a spectacular setting. The rock formation on the left looks like my idea of the garden tomb."

"Doesn't it? I get chills just thinking about it."

Jason took Mary's hand as they walked down the rough-hewn steps to the bottom of the hill. They looked out in silence over the valley below for a moment before returning to the car.

"I'm surprised this area isn't covered with houses," Jason said.

"We can thank Congressman Winter and his Warren kin for that. They still own a lot of the land and want to keep the top pretty much as it was when their Cherokee ancestors hid out here instead of being forced to walk the Trail of Tears."

"I understand Hawk Henson's ancestors came here for the same reason," Jason said.

"Some Cherokee living around the Tennessee River were rounded up, but others saw what was going on in time to get to the mountains. They had hunted here, and they knew no one would likely bother to look for them in this wilderness."

"That Native American removal was a terrible business," Jason said. "Now I've seen Warren Mountain, I'd like to take a look at that ridge on the opposite side of town."

"It's called Oliver Mountain." From his smile, Mary decided Jason must already know that.

"Were your folks running from the soldiers' roundup, too?" Jason asked.

"No. Both sides of my family were living in Virginia in the late sixteen hundreds. They moved to North Carolina and Georgia before settling here around 1830. How about your family?"

"The Abbotts were English, but I don't know much more than that."

They reached the base of Warren Mountain, and Mary directed Jason to the street leading to the winding Oliver Mountain road.

"I don't see houses on this ridge, either," Jason observed as they neared the summit.

"Not now. The first Oliver and Austin families lived up here, but after a fire in the late eighteen hundreds, my great-grandfather moved off the mountain and built the house we live in now. Our family cemetery is here, so we'll never sell off any of our part."

"You don't own it all?"

"No. My mother's people, the Austins, had the parcel overlooking Rockdale."

When they reached the crest of the ridge, Jason parked the car and he and Mary walked into the cemetery. "What a great last resting place—I know it takes hard work to keep a place like this up."

"Our relatives get together and clean it each Decoration Day, and my father and I work on it at times during the year."

"Tell me about the people buried here." Jason's tone indicated his interest, and Mary led him to the headstones Todd Walker had recently cleaned.

"Warren and Mary Austin were my great-great-great-grandparents on my mother's side. Theirs are the oldest graves here. Their daughter married the first Wayne Oliver. He and his wife are buried over there."

"What about all these smaller headstones?"

"Infants and small children. Many died young in the early days."

Jason stroked the weathered head of a cherub above a small child's grave. "After all these years, it's still sad to see these."

" 'The Lord giveth, and the Lord taketh away, blessed be the name of the Lord,' " Mary read aloud from an adjacent headstone.

"At least they had a strong faith. That's a great heritage for any family."

When they finished walking around the graves, Mary pointed to the road leading to the end of the ridge. "You can see a lot of Rockdale from here."

"Should I get the car?" Jason asked.

"No, it's an easy walk, but we need to take precautions against chigoes. The spray is in my purse."

"It seems I have a lot to learn about country life."

"Chigoes are good teachers." Mary used the spray and handed it to Jason.

Thus prepared, they started walking, and Jason again took Mary's hand. When they reached the meadow where she and Walter Chance had recently stood, Mary stopped short and put her free hand to her throat. Pink plastic ribbons fluttered from the top of a series of wooden surveyor's stakes.

"These stakes weren't here last week."

"It looks like somebody may be planning to build up here."

"I don't know why—the meadow is too far from the edge to get the benefit of the view."

"Who owns this land?"

Mary shook her head. "I don't really know—it's passed through many hands in the past century." *But this is Austin land, and Todd Walker's mother was an Austin.*

"Where's the view of the town you mentioned?"

"To the right—we're almost there." Disturbed by what she had just seen, Mary led Jason to the edge of the bluff. *I must find out who made that survey.*

"Wow," Jason said when they reached the edge.

Although Mary had seen the sight numerous times, she felt the same way. She pointed to the spire of First Church and the dome of the courthouse, both almost hidden by surrounding trees. "After the leaves fall, you can see much more."

"It's like looking down at the land when you first take off in an airplane." After a moment, Jason glanced at the ground and kicked at a loose rock beside his foot. "Anyone living here would have a spectacular view, but this rock outcropping would be expensive to build on."

Mary didn't repeat Walter's opinion that the land was suited for a quarry. *The less said about him, the better.*

"Not only that—I'd rather look up at the mountain and see

trees than a house." *Or a quarry.*

"So would I. What else do you suggest I should see today?"

"Pastor Hurley probably took you out Rockdale Boulevard. Did he say anything about the ridge where it dead ends?"

"No. Is it special?"

"It could be." Mary repeated what Todd Walker said about adding a connecting road and developing the land around it.

"That would cost a ton of money. Who would pay for it?"

"Someone who thought the return would be worth it, I suppose. I can't imagine what Rockdale would be like if that happened."

Jason smiled faintly. "You sound like someone who wants things to stay the way they are."

"Some things."

"From what I heard last night, that might not be possible."

"I know, but I like Rockdale the way it is now."

"So do I. At least I like what I've seen so far."

Jason's smile made his comment personal. Flustered, Mary turned from the bluff. "We should go now. DeSoto fills up early for lunch this time of year."

❧

On the drive out of town, Jason asked Mary about the school system.

"Rockdale isn't perfect, but it's a good place for children to grow up," Mary concluded.

"With teachers like you, I can see why."

Jason spoke so matter-of-factly Mary didn't think he meant to flatter her, as Walter Chance seemed so fond of doing. Mary admitted Jason's comment probably meant more to her than it should have, and she could think of no adequate reply. "You've never seen me teach," she finally said.

"I don't have to. Your eyes light up when you talk about children, and I've noticed the way you interact with them. All the programs in the world mean nothing if the teacher doesn't love children."

"Like 'a resounding gong or a clanging cymbal'?" Mary

quoted from 1 Corinthians 13.

Jason nodded. "Exactly."

They were still talking easily when they entered DeSoto Park Lodge, and Mary realized there had been no awkward silences between them. Even when neither spoke, the time between their conversations seemed comfortable.

Dining room hostess Sally Morgan raised her eyebrows when Mary and Jason entered. "Hello, Pastor Jason. Hi, Mary."

"Hello, Mrs. Morgan. Mary's been helping me plan the children's program at church. As I mentioned the other day, Pastor Hurley and I hope you and Ted will work with us on it."

Sally shrugged. "My husband doesn't think he can teach little children. He's afraid he'd be out of place."

"I disagree. Tell Ted we'll talk about it soon."

"That would help." Sally Morgan smiled slightly as she reverted to her hostess role. "Do y'all want the buffet today?"

"Yes, we do."

"Since it's not raining, you can have a window table."

"What did she mean by that?" Jason asked after they were seated.

"Sally knows I stay away from windows during storms."

"Another good idea. Maybe I should start writing them down."

Mary replied in the same light tone. "I don't think anyone would want them."

"That's their loss. I know a good thing when I see it."

Mary accepted his words as friendly banter. After all, a man like Jason who was engaged to one woman wouldn't seriously compliment another.

⁂

Jason had never seen Lodge Falls, so after they ate, Mary took him on the now-familiar path. She felt a strong sense of déjà vu as they stood together and watched the water for a while, then sat in silence on the same bench she'd recently shared with Todd Walker.

Jason had held her hand on the path, but he released it

when they were seated. He looked out over the water as if not really seeing it, and Mary wondered what he was thinking.

As easy as conversation between them had been, Jason had said little about his personal life and nothing at all about his fiancée. After sitting beside him in silence for some time, Mary decided their friendship allowed her to bring up the subject.

"I hope your fiancée will like Rockdale."

Jason looked startled. "My fiancée?"

"The woman you plan to marry. Everyone says you're engaged."

Jason's brow furrowed and he shook his head. "I'm sorry about that. It was all a misunderstanding."

"You thought you were engaged but you're not?"

"No. I mean I'm not engaged, and I never was. When Pastor Hurley interviewed me, he asked if I planned to marry and I said I did. I meant it in general terms, but he took it to mean I was already committed to someone."

But he's not. Jason Abbott isn't taken, after all! Mary's heart soared. "That must have been embarrassing."

"It was. Especially last Sunday when they ordered a corsage for my nonexistent fiancée."

"What did you tell them?"

"I left it up to Pastor Hurley. He decided against making a public announcement, but if anyone asks, he confirms I'm not engaged."

"That should make a lot of Community Church women glad."

Mary's tone was light, but Jason's response wasn't.

"I told Pastor Hurley the truth. I believe God's plan for my life includes marriage and a family someday."

Mary's sincerity matched his. "Then He will let you know when that time comes."

"How about you? Do you believe God really wants you to remain single?"

His question caught Mary off guard. "I told you I was

called to be a teacher. I haven't heard any further call."

"I wonder if you're listening."

Jason's query made Mary uncomfortable. "I—I hope so."

"I would have said the same thing once. When I was in college, I wanted a career in business so much I didn't ask if God approved. When I landed a high-paying position with a big firm in Atlanta as soon as I graduated, I took it as a sign God blessed my choice."

"Obviously, you changed your mind," Mary said after a moment.

"No, God changed it for me. It didn't take me long to realize I'd always be miserable doing what I wanted. From the moment I gave Him all my life and sought His will in everything, God began to lead me into the ministry. The journey hasn't always been easy, but I felt His presence every step of the way."

"I always wanted to be a teacher," Mary said. "I felt that calling so strongly I never even considered doing anything else."

"That doesn't mean God doesn't have something else in store for you. Three months ago, I'd never heard of Rockdale, yet here I am. I believe it's for a reason."

"So do I," Mary murmured.

Jason stood, signaling his readiness to leave. On the drive back to Rockdale, he described some of the part-time jobs he'd had while attending seminary, and Mary told him about the mission trips she'd taken while in college.

"At one time I thought of becoming a missionary, but God didn't open those doors, so I came back here."

"From all reports, your Rockdale first-graders are your mission field."

Mary smiled faintly. "That sounds like Toni Trent. She thinks of her work for Rock County in the same way."

"She's not the only one. Anita Sanchez—I mean Henson—can't say enough nice things about you. But even before they said anything, I knew from Ann you had a special gift for working with children."

"No, it's the other way around. The students I teach and the children at First are a precious gift. I try to do my best for them."

"I know—it shows."

The admiration in his voice embarrassed Mary, and as much as she had enjoyed being with Jason, she was glad they had reached her house. She thanked him for lunch and automatically invited him to come inside. He politely declined, then surprised Mary by shaking her hand.

"Thanks for the tour and for all the other help. You don't know how much I value your friendship."

Jason's words cut Mary as no knife could have. She wanted to tell him she was willing to be more than his friend, but he was gone before she could frame the words.

As she closed the door, Mary imagined what Sally Proffitt might tell Jenny Suiter this time. *From the way they shook hands when he brought her home, I'd say nothing's going on between Mary Oliver and that new Pastor Abbott, after all.*

twenty

Mary was still going over every detail of her day with Jason Abbott when Walter Chance called to say he'd pick her up at five o'clock.

Jarred back to the present, Mary spoke more harshly than her conscience liked. "No, you won't. I tried to tell you at Statum's I couldn't go."

"I guess I didn't hear you." Walter paused. "Are you all right? You sound funny."

I feel funny, too. "I'm fine, but I won't go out with you again, so please don't ask."

"Is it the judge? I thought he liked me."

He probably likes you better than I do. However, Mary resolved to be kind. "My father believes you have a good head on your shoulders. Maybe you can help solve a mystery."

Walter sounded bewildered. "The way you're acting is a mystery to me."

"Who put those survey stakes on Oliver Mountain?"

Walter's slight hesitation spoke volumes. "What stakes?"

"I think you know."

"Don't worry about it."

"Walter Chance, don't try to hold out on me."

He laughed ruefully. "I'm not. I planned to tell you about it at dinner tonight."

It was Mary's turn to hesitate, but only momentarily. "Tell me what? If you know anything about Oliver Mountain, you should share it."

"That's what I was trying to do. Are you sure you can't go tonight?"

I won't go, not just can't. "I'm positive. Good-bye, Walter."

Mary hung up the receiver before Walter could say anything else.

When her father came home, Mary told him about the stakes she'd seen that morning.

"That's odd. Why would anyone survey that land?"

Mary debated how to tell her father the little she knew. "The stakes are on the meadow side, not the bluff. I'm beginning to believe Walter knows more about several things than he's told us."

"Such as?"

"Apparently he bid on the bluff land around Mentone that Todd Walker's company bought. I wouldn't be surprised if he's already taken options on the land at the foot of Rockdale Ridge."

Wayne Oliver looked thoughtful. "I suppose that might explain why he's pushing new zoning laws, but he agrees there can't be a quarry on Oliver Mountain."

"If you ask him about the stakes, he'll probably tell you what he knows."

"I want to see them for myself. Do you want to go with me?"

"No, thanks. I'll stay here and start supper. You'll need the bug spray—it's in my purse. Jason and I used it this morning."

Her father shook his head. "Jason Abbott, Todd Walker, Walter Chance—you're always going out with some man or the other these days."

"It only seems that way. Anyway, it doesn't mean anything."

He looked thoughtful. "Maybe it will. You know I'd like to see you marry."

So would I. Mary's realization she didn't want the Oliver line and heritage to end with her had been slow to come, but now Mary felt ready to welcome marriage—if it was in God's plan.

"I suppose stranger things have happened," she said.

❧

Shortly after her father left, the telephone rang.

"I hope I didn't catch you at a bad time," Todd Walker said.

What does he want? "I'm about to start supper."

"I'm sure it'll be something good."

"Join us if you're in Rockdale."

"Unfortunately, I'm not. I have business in Rockdale tomorrow, though. I'd like to see you."

"Why?"

"Do I need a reason to want to see you?"

No, but I'd like to know what you're really up to. "What time?"

"Around noon."

"All right."

Todd's tone lightened. "I like a woman of few words. I'll see you tomorrow."

Mary returned to her supper preparations, her mind in turmoil. She should be happy Todd Walker wanted to see her. Why, then, didn't she look forward to meeting him again?

❧

Over supper, Mary's father told her what he'd found.

"The stakes you saw today have nothing to do with the bluff property. I intend to find out why they're there."

"Walter didn't say who owns the meadow land. Do you know?"

"Yes."

"Care to share it with me?"

"Not just yet."

"I almost forgot—Todd Walker called while you were gone. He's coming to Rockdale on business tomorrow."

Her father raised his eyebrows. "Really? Have him call me. We have some matters to discuss."

❧

Mary didn't care to be seen with Todd Walker at Statum's, nor did she want to go out of town for lunch again. Instead, she put together chicken salad, fruit trifle, and orange mint tea and set the kitchen table with the everyday stoneware.

She doubted Todd Walker had come to Rockdale to see her, but when Mary opened the door to him, she realized anew how handsome he was. *Any woman ought to be proud to be seen with such a man.*

"Come in," Mary invited.

"No—come out and we'll go to lunch," he countered.

"We're eating here. I hope you like chicken salad."

"I do, but I planned to take you somewhere special."

"Too late! Your lunch awaits. We'll eat in the kitchen—you can wash your hands at the sink," she said cheerfully.

Mary feared she might have overdone being casual, but Todd didn't seem to mind. "I enjoy being treated like home folks."

"You are. After all, we're kin."

Todd smiled when she offered him a towel to dry his hands. "Kissing kin." He bent his head and brushed her lips lightly. "That's the best kind."

Without comment, Mary took her place at the table and offered grace.

"That was nice," he said, and Mary suspected it had been a long time since he had heard thanks returned.

"How did your business go?" she asked.

"Very well. It's not official yet, so you're the first to know. After I told my bosses Rockdale will support it, Haskell Holdings agreed to build a recreation complex at the foot of Rockdale Ridge."

"Something like that is certainly needed," Mary said.

While he ate, Todd spoke glowingly of the plans for a swimming pool, lighted tennis courts, and all-purpose recreation center.

A suspicion dawned in Mary's mind. "You must have been working on this for a long time." *That's the real reason you came here on Decoration Day.*

Todd tried to sound modest. "Other people had already drawn up preliminary plans. I helped site the final design."

And I suppose you also promised to get local approval, starting with the help of the influential Judge Oliver. "It seems you've earned another feather in your cap."

"That remains to be seen." He leaned back in his chair and smiled at her. "I don't know which was better, the food or sharing it with you."

That sounds a lot like something Walter Chance would say. "Are you ready for the garden tour now?" Mary asked.

"Later. I want you to see something. Get your hat and let's go."

Seems to me I've heard that before. Mary glanced at her sandals and sighed. "I'll change shoes and be right back."

❧

Todd was driving his truck, and Mary felt a sense of déjà vu when he turned onto the winding Oliver Mountain road.

"Are we going to the cemetery?" she asked.

"No."

Without comment, Todd drove to the edge of the meadow, where several sets of tire tracks gave evidence of recent activity in the area. As Todd helped Mary from the truck, the sun went behind a dark cloud and the survey markers' plastic streamers danced in the freshening breeze.

Mary shivered and Todd put his arm around her shoulders. "I used to play here in this meadow on Decoration Days while my folks worked in the cemetery."

"What do you know about these stakes?" she asked.

Instead of answering her question, Todd countered with another. "Look around, Mary. What do you see?"

"A flat meadow and a rocky bluff. Why?"

"From a height of twenty-five feet, the view of Rockdale would be terrific—the whole town would be at your feet."

Mary voiced her suspicion. "Does Haskell Holdings have something to do with these stakes?"

Todd sounded astonished. "Of course not. Why would you think that?"

"You work for them."

"Yes, but that's not why I had this plat surveyed. Don't you see? It's the perfect place for a house."

Mary felt confused. "I didn't know you owned this land."

"I don't."

"Who does?"

"You really don't know?"

Mary slowly shook her head. In the distance, thunder rolled. A hawk wheeled overhead, and somewhere a crow called. It seemed a very long time before Todd spoke.

"You do, Mary. Marry me, and I'll build you the finest house Rockdale's ever seen."

twenty-one

Mary felt stunned. "If this is your idea of a joke—"

Todd pulled Mary to him and kissed her. "I've never been more serious about anything in my life. How about it?"

Mary detached herself from his embrace and stepped back a few paces. "I know it's a cliché, but this really is sudden. We barely know each other."

"I know all I need to about you, and if you want more time to get to know me, that's fine—it'll take some time to choose a plan and build the house, anyway."

Thunder sounded again, nearer and louder, and the wind bore the scent of rain. Todd took Mary's hand. "Let's go back to the truck before we get soaked."

The moment they got inside, heavy rain began to beat a tattoo upon the roof. "This reminds me of sleeping under Grandma Austin's tin roof as a kid," Todd said. "I hoped it would rain every time I stayed there."

Mary heard Todd speaking, but she scarcely took in what he was saying. She didn't know which was more preposterous, Todd Walker's sudden proposal of marriage or the revelation he wanted to build a house on land he apparently thought she owned.

There has to be something more than love behind this proposal.

"Aren't you going to say anything?" Todd asked after a while.

"You don't like chatterboxes," Mary reminded him.

Todd took her hand, the only contact the truck's center console allowed. "A simple 'yes' will do. How about it?"

"Not until you explain a few things."

Todd sighed. "I'll admit I haven't always been a saint, but I turned over a new leaf when I came back to Alabama. Now I

156

want to settle down with you and raise a family in the place where I was born. What else do you need to know?"

It would help if you could say you loved me. "The rain's letting up—please take me home."

⋆

Todd matched Mary's silence on the way back to her house. He drove his truck to the rear of the house and walked Mary to the door.

"When can I see you again?" he asked.

"I don't know. I need to talk to my father."

Todd grinned unexpectedly. "That's supposed to be my line. You're really something, Miss Mary Oliver. I'll call you tomorrow."

Mary closed the kitchen door and sighed. *He won't be coming back. Or if he does, I won't see him. I no longer have a crush on you, Todd Walker.*

Feeling strangely detached, Mary went to her room and examined her reflection in her dresser mirror. She didn't look different, but she felt greatly changed by the last few weeks. She glanced at the yellowed index card she'd tucked in the mirror frame years before: "The Lord does not look at the things man looks at. Man looks at the outward appearance, but the Lord looks at the heart."

Once she had used the Scripture to help her feel better about herself. Now, the familiar words had new meaning. Todd Walker's appearance was handsome, all right, but Mary believed the praise of men mattered too much to him.

On the other hand, no one could accuse the usually disheveled Jason Abbott of vanity. His priorities obviously centered more on the spiritual side of life than on the material.

Mary tried to picture herself as Jason might, a dedicated teacher who loves children. But he'd told Mary to listen for God to tell her if His will for her life included something more.

Turning from the mirror, Mary knelt beside her bed. Her standard, general prayer for guidance seemed somehow hollow. Recalling Jason's experience, Mary realized what had been missing from her own petitions.

Lord, I've been too busy thinking I'm doing Your will to listen to You. I thank You for using Jason Abbott to speak that truth to me. Forgive me for my presumption and for all the many other ways I have failed You. I promise to be a better listener, and I ask You to show me what I should do and trust You to help me do it.

❧

Some time later, the telephone rang. Mary was going to let the answering machine take the call, but when she heard her father's voice, she picked up the receiver.

"Is Todd still there?"

"No. He left some time ago. I'm sorry, I forgot to give him your message."

"I'm on my way home. We need to talk."

❧

Her father found Mary in the living room and wasted no time telling her what he'd discovered.

"Todd hired the survey crew that put those stakes on the mountain."

"I know. He told me."

"Did he say why?"

"He wants to build a house there."

Her father looked shocked. *"What?* He doesn't even own that land."

"Who does, then?"

Wayne Oliver sighed. "It was originally Austin land. Your grandfather Austin put the meadow lot in trust for your mother and her heirs when she was born. After her death, some of the other Austins wanted to add their shares to yours and develop it, but they couldn't touch it as long as it was in the trust."

"Why didn't you tell me?"

"I should have, of course. I didn't think you'd want to sell the land, although by the terms of the trust you'd gain control of it on attaining the age of thirty."

Which I just did. "Todd obviously knows about the trust. Who else does?"

Her father shrugged. "Anyone with the patience to dig into the probate records, I suppose."

"Walter Chance," Mary murmured. "I think he must have found out, too. I don't believe anyone ever intended to put a rock quarry on Oliver Mountain. He wanted to make sure the land would be taken into the city and zoned residential so he could develop it himself."

"Aren't you jumping to conclusions? How would Walter get the land?"

"The same way as Todd—by marrying me."

Wayne Oliver looked stunned. "I knew Walter was leaning that way, but Todd? He actually asked you to marry him?"

"Hard to believe, isn't it? Walter hasn't gotten down on bended knee, but he's dropped some heavy hints. Todd proposed to me today on top of Oliver Mountain. What will you do about his survey?"

He shrugged. "Nothing, I suppose. The property isn't posted, and it's not illegal to survey someone else's land. Margaret Hastings complimented Todd—she said he's worked hard to persuade Haskell Holdings to build a recreation and entertainment complex in Rockdale."

Mary nodded. "I know, and the town needs it."

Her father looked at Mary closely. "Are you positive you don't want to marry Todd? I know you once liked him a great deal."

So he knew I had a crush on Todd, after all. "He said he wants to settle down in Rockdale and have a family. I felt comfortable with him before today, but I can't agree to a marriage based on deceit."

"All right. If Todd should ask about the land—"

"You can tell him it's not for sale," Mary said firmly.

❧

After the whirlwind of activity of the past few weeks, Mary should have welcomed the opportunity to do as little as she wanted, but she felt at loose ends all weekend. Vacation Bible School wouldn't start for ten days, the ground was too wet for gardening, and none of the books Mary tried to read held her interest.

When Walter called on Saturday, Mary told him the mystery of the stakes had been solved. "No one will be building anything on that land anytime soon."

"That's really a pity. You could have a beautiful view from the second story."

Mary hung up, shaking her head. She held nothing against Walter, and she hoped with all her heart he'd find someone to share his life—but it wouldn't be her.

Todd called later to apologize for the way he'd bungled his proposal. "Will you give me another chance? I'll be in Rockdale often, and I hope you'll agree to continue to see me."

"It wouldn't do either of us any good. I wish you well with the recreation project, but that's it."

Todd sounded genuinely sorry. "If you change your mind, you know how to reach me."

Yes, Todd, I have your number—in more ways than one.

The only man Mary really wanted to hear from did not call. At the very least, she hoped Jason Abbott would continue to ask her advice, but with every passing day even that seemed more unlikely. Word of his availability had gotten out, and everywhere Mary went in the next week she heard wild suppositions about why Jason and his fiancée had broken up, coupled with speculation about the women he might date now that he was "free."

Mary kept silent, not wishing to add fuel to a fire that was obviously already out of control. Again she thought of how the New Testament writer James had compared the tongue to a flame of fire. *When it's used to gossip, it can certainly destroy lives.*

Her father spent much of his free time that week attending various committee meetings of the Rockdale Civic Improvement Association and working with city council members on zoning laws and similar matters.

After what seemed a very long week, Mary held a final Vacation Bible School planning meeting on a cloudy Friday afternoon. After the others left, Mary entered the sanctuary. The moment she walked in, Mary realized she wasn't alone.

Jason Abbott rose from a pew nearest the Oliver stained glass window. "Hello, Mary. I hope I didn't startle you."

"What are you doing here?" She blurted out the words, then tried to soften her reaction. "Obviously, you're looking at our windows."

"Actually, I came to see you, but I couldn't resist studying this stained glass again. It's surprising how much light filters through it even on a cloudy day."

"Yes. You wanted to see me?"

"Your father said you were here. I want to ask a favor."

Anything. Say it and if it's in my power, I'll do it. "What is it?"

"I know your Vacation Bible School starts on Monday. I'd like to visit from time to time and see what you're doing."

"Of course. I assume you're still looking for ideas for Community's Bible school?"

Jason smiled faintly. "I've been nicely told plans have already been made for this year, but I'm looking ahead."

"I have no idea how all the new things we're trying will work out, but you're welcome to come by to observe any time."

"Thanks. I look forward to it."

They stood together beside the window, outlined in the colored light filtering in through the stained glass. Jason had said what he had come to say, and their business was over. Mary knew she should leave, yet she was reluctant to do so.

"How are things going at Community?" she asked.

Jason smiled ruefully. "I suppose you're aware each of us has been the talk of the town this week. I'll be glad when some other topic for gossip comes along."

Each of us? "What have you heard about me?"

Jason's smile faded. "I shouldn't have said anything. I don't like to repeat gossip."

"Now that you've brought it up you have to tell me."

He sighed. "The word is you're about to get married."

"I am? To whom?"

"There's some disagreement. Some say Walter Chance, others Todd something—he spoke a long time at the meeting last week."

"Todd Walker," Mary supplied. "How do these wild stories get started?"

"You're not engaged?"

"No more than you were. I've heard several versions of why your fiancée broke off your engagement, by the way."

Jason smiled. "I won't believe what I hear about you if you'll do the same for me."

Mary smiled. "Agreed."

Jason lightly touched Mary's cheek. "I'm glad the gossips were wrong."

Her heart lurched, then began to beat more rapidly. "So am I."

"I have to get back to work, but I hope to see you soon."

He really seems to mean it. Thank You, Lord.

twenty-two

Rain fell the first two days of Vacation Bible School, preventing the planned Nature Walks, but it still went smoothly. The weather didn't seem to affect the turnout for the second Rockdale Civic Improvement Association general meeting Tuesday evening, and Wayne Oliver seemed satisfied at the work that was being accomplished.

Jason wasn't at the meeting, and although Mary watched for him daily, she didn't see him again until near the end of Wednesday's Vacation Bible School session. After the children had been dismissed, he invited Mary to lunch.

"I'm sorry I couldn't get here sooner, but this has been a busy week. I brought a picnic lunch. I'll let you decide where we should take it."

Mary tried not to sound quite as joyful as she felt. "I know a great spot on Warren Mountain."

Mary directed Jason to an old logging road, from which they walked into a grassy meadow surrounded by wildflowers.

"Don't I hear water?" Jason asked.

"That's the everlasting spring. It appears to come out of the mountain and makes a neat little waterfall before it goes down the mountain and becomes the creek we cross to get into town. We can eat on the big rocks around it if you like."

"I brought a tarp, but this is much better."

When they were settled on the rocks, Jason opened a huge hamper filled with containers of food and bottles of water and soda. "Everything but the ants," he said when Mary commented on the seemingly endless supply of food. "My neighbor, Mrs. Tarpley, fried the chicken and made the brownies. The rest is straight from the grocery."

"Partaking of God's bounty surrounded by God's beauty.

163

I can't think of a nicer way to have lunch," Mary said.

"Neither can I." Jason took her hand and offered a prayer of thanks for all God's gifts, particularly for their fellowship and the food that had been prepared for them.

"Amen," Mary echoed when he finished.

Jason seemed reluctant to release Mary's hand. "This is a perfect place for a picnic. How did you find it?"

"Toni Trent and I rode our bikes up here quite often when we were in Rockdale High."

"You two have been friends a long time," Jason observed.

"Yes. In fact, we were the only friends each other had in those days."

"It's hard to believe you and Toni weren't popular."

"About as popular as poison ivy. How about you? Were you voted the most anything when you were in school?"

"No. I felt awkward and ugly, so I made good grades instead of friends. I thought if I could earn a lot of money, everybody would like me."

Jason spoke matter-of-factly, but Mary understood the hurt he must have known. "Except for the money part, I felt the same way."

"My mother kept telling me I should look at myself through God's eyes and not my own or others'. Now I realize how self-centered I was then," Jason said.

"I know what you mean. I relied on the verse in First Samuel 'Man looks at the outward appearance, but the Lord looks at the heart.'"

Jason spoke quietly. "When I look at you, I see a beautiful woman whose life reflects her love for God and His children."

Beautiful. No one had ever called Mary beautiful, and she tried to hide the depth of her pleasure.

"That's a fine compliment, but it doesn't sound like you're talking about me."

"Don't sell yourself short, Mary. I know God doesn't."

When they had finished eating, Jason took Mary's hands in his and looked into her eyes. "Have you given any more thought about what God wants for your life?"

Mary's gaze held his. "I've been praying about it."

"Good." Jason squeezed Mary's hands, then released them and picked up the picnic hamper. "I wish I didn't have to go back to work this afternoon. We'll have to do this again."

Soon, I hope. "Don't forget you're invited to the Vacation Bible School field trip on Friday."

"I haven't—and you can be sure if I'm not there, it won't be because I didn't want to be."

&

Mary's prayers for a successful and safe trip to Sequoyah Caverns were answered. The hired buses got the children there and back on time without breaking down, and everything else went off as planned. Awed by the beauty of the cave's lake and gigantic rock formations, the kids behaved well.

Mary's only regret was that Jason Abbott wasn't there to enjoy it with them.

"Thank you for arranging this trip for us," Mary told Hawk Henson at the end of the day. "Seeing God's handiwork here capped off the whole week. This place is truly inspirational. I'm glad the Cherokee own at least this part of your ancestral land."

"So are we. I'm sorry Pastor Jason couldn't get away today. He's interested in planning a trip like this for our church's kids."

"I'll be glad to show it to him later."

Hawk remained silent for a moment. "It's too bad you're so committed to First Church. You and Pastor Jason would make a great team at Community."

I believe we could make a good team, period. "We're sharing information and programs as it is."

But after Mary got home that night, she considered Hawk's remark. *It's too bad you're so committed to First Church.*

Mary wondered if Jason Abbot might have had the same thought. First Church had always been at the heart of her spiritual life, but she recognized it was only a building. *Its purpose is to help people worship God—and since He exists in Spirit and in Truth and not in bricks and stones and glass, I should never let it take the place of God.*

Mary now believed Jason Abbott had entered her life for a reason, but she wasn't so sure about what role, if any, she was meant play in his. That night when she knelt to pray, Mary acknowledged her future still seemed in doubt.

Lord, I am wholly committed to You. You know how much I love First Church, but I love You more. If it is Your will for me to help Your servant Jason in his church, I will obey.

❧

Jason called Mary on Saturday to get her version of the field trip. "According to Hawk, it was a great success. He thinks Community should do the same for our Bible school."

"I'm sorry you couldn't come with us, but I'll be happy to take you to the caverns when you have time."

"Thanks—I'd like that. We've been busy preparing for the Fourth of July celebration. Toni will sing a solo, and after the service, we'll have an old-fashioned dinner on the grounds. I wish you could be here for it."

"Is that an invitation?"

"Yes, but I know you'll probably have obligations at First, particularly on the first Sunday after Bible school."

"Yes. I'm due to give the Vacation Bible School report to the church. Maybe some other time."

Jason sounded resigned. " 'Never the twain shall meet,' " he quoted.

Mary hesitated. "Never is a long time. Good-bye, Jason."

❧

On Sunday morning, Mary's father showed her the ring he intended to give Evelyn when they went to Mentone for lunch after church.

Mary admired the emerald-cut diamond set in white gold. "Does she know about this?"

"No. When she agreed to be my wife, Evelyn said she didn't need an engagement ring. However, I want her to have one."

"She'll love it." When Mary hugged her father, unexpected tears gathered in her eyes.

"Hey, you're not supposed to cry until the wedding," he said.

Mary smiled. "I'll probably cry then, too."

As soon as she reached the church, Mary sought out Melanie Neal. "I know it's short notice, but will you please read the Vacation Bible School report at the worship service?"

Melanie looked mystified. "You always give the report. It's your big moment."

"Not this time. I have something more important to do."

ख

Mary walked into Community Church on legs that seemed to have turned to jelly. Anita Henson saw her and took Mary's hand.

"Toni will be so happy you have come to hear her sing," she said.

Mary nodded, grateful for the excuse.

At their invitation, Mary sat between Anita and her daughter, who seemed delighted to see her. Hawk grinned and gave Mary the thumbs-up sign.

Hawk seems to understand why I'm here today. Will Jason?

The service began, and from his chair near the pulpit Jason glanced idly over the congregation. When he saw Mary, he did a double take, then smiled.

Mary felt a surge of joy. *He's glad I'm here—and so am I.*

Community's informal worship service was different from First's in many ways, but Mary realized everything that really mattered was the same. Like First Church, Community consisted of a body of believers, united as brothers and sisters in Jesus Christ.

While Pastor Hurley prayed, Mary's mind and heart overflowed with praise, not only for all God had given her, but also for what He yet had in store.

After the benediction, Jason hurried to find Mary and took her arm.

"Where are you going, Pastor Jason?" little Juanita asked.

"We're s'posed to eat now."

"Later. Miss Mary and I have to talk first."

Dimly aware of the curious glances they attracted, Mary allowed Jason to lead her through the hallway and into his office. He closed the door behind him and turned to her.

"What about your report?"

"I asked someone else to read it. I'm sure First Church is still standing."

"Even without one of its pillars?"

"God has let me know I can be a pillar anywhere He wants to use me."

"Even here?"

"Especially here."

"Hallelujah!" Jason's face broke into the widest smile Mary had ever seen just before he swept her into his arms and kissed her.

Still holding her tight, he whispered in her ear, "I pray God has also let you know you should marry me."

She pulled away to look at him. "Without first being asked?"

"Of course not, if you think it's necessary." Jason took her right hand in his and looked intently into her eyes. "Mary Oliver, I love you and I want to be your best friend, your life's partner, and your husband—as long as we both shall live."

"Amen," said Mary. "In that case, the answer has to be a yes."

"Thank You, Lord," he whispered, then kissed her again.

Folded in Jason Abbott's arms, Mary felt as if she'd come home after a long journey. She had no doubt God had led them both to this moment—and her to this man.

Thank You for helping me to make the right choice.

epilogue

Everyone agreed Rockdale had never experienced such a summer. With the help of the Civic Improvement Association, new zoning laws were put into place to protect the town's natural beauty. Several projects which would offer more shopping, dining, and recreation choices and add tax revenue were in the works, and Haskell Holdings held a gala ground-breaking ceremony for the entertainment and recreation center. It was no wonder the entire town felt a sense of optimism.

The summer also brought changes in the personal lives of several Rockdale residents. Walter Chance had helped a pretty young widow with three children find a house, and soon it seemed evident they might be headed for the altar.

Todd Walker continued to work for Haskell Holdings. Still single, he had apparently dropped his plans to settle down in Rockdale.

Mary Oliver created quite a stir when she joined Community Church, and she and the associate pastor were seen together quite often. After Jason Abbott took Mary to Georgia to meet his parents, no one was surprised when their engagement was announced, with plans for a late December wedding.

After a short engagement, Judge Wayne Oliver and Miss Evelyn Trent were married at First Church in a simple but moving service. After the Olivers returned from their honeymoon cruise, Evelyn moved out of her house on Maple Street, and Mary moved into it.

On the day Evelyn's furniture arrived at its new home in the Oliver house, she and Mary noticed Sally Proffitt and Jenny Suiter watching from Sally's porch.

"Those poor ladies will have to find someone new to gossip about now, now that I'm married and you're engaged," Evelyn said.

"What they really need is to feel useful. Jason's asked Phyllis Dickson to involve them in some kind of volunteer work at the hospital."

"Good. Your Pastor Jason seems to have a gift for knowing exactly what people need."

"He does, doesn't he? I hadn't thought of that as one of his gifts, but it is."

"You know, it wasn't an accident you two found each other," Evelyn said. "Jason needed someone to support his ministry, and you needed to be a wife as well as a teacher."

"God knew I needed a stepmother like you, too—I really believe you and my father were meant to be together."

Evelyn smiled. "Isn't it amazing how—when we let Him—God leads us to make the right choices?"

A Letter To Our Readers

Dear Reader:

In order that we might better contribute to your reading enjoyment, we would appreciate your taking a few minutes to respond to the following questions. We welcome your comments and read each form and letter we receive. When completed, please return to the following:

Fiction Editor
Heartsong Presents
PO Box 719
Uhrichsville, Ohio 44683

1. Did you enjoy reading *Mary's Choice* by Kay Cornelius?
   ❑ Very much! I would like to see more books by this author!
   ❑ Moderately. I would have enjoyed it more if

   _____

   _____

   _____

2. Are you a member of **Heartsong Presents**? ❑ Yes ❑ No
   If no, where did you purchase this book? _____

   _____

3. How would you rate, on a scale from 1 (poor) to 5 (superior), the cover design? _____

4. On a scale from 1 (poor) to 10 (superior), please rate the following elements.

   ____ Heroine   ____ Plot
   ____ Hero   ____ Inspirational theme
   ____ Setting   ____ Secondary characters

5. These characters were special because?_____

_____

_____

6. How has this book inspired your life?_____

_____

_____

7. What settings would you like to see covered in future
   Heartsong Presents books? _____

_____

_____

8. What are some inspirational themes you would like to see
   treated in future books? _____

_____

_____

9. Would you be interested in reading other **Heartsong
   Presents** titles? ❑ Yes ❑ No

10. Please check your age range:
   ❑ Under 18   ❑ 18-24
   ❑ 25-34   ❑ 35-45
   ❑ 46-55   ❑ Over 55

Name_____

Occupation _____

Address _____

City_____ State_____ Zip_____

Sweet Treats

4 stories in 1

*T*hese four complete novels follow the culinary adventures—and misadventures—of Cynthia and three of her culinary students who want to stir up a little romance.

Four seasoned authors blend their skills in this delightful compilation: Wanda E. Brunstetter, Birdie L. Etchison, Pamela Griffin, and Tamela Hancock Murray.

Contemporary, paperback, 368 pages, 5 ³/₁₆" x 8"

❤ ❤ ❤ ❤ ❤ ❤ ❤ ❤ ❤ ❤ ❤ ❤ ❤ ❤ ❤ ❤ ❤

Please send me _____ copies of *Sweet Treats*. I am enclosing $6.97 for each. (Please add $2.00 to cover postage and handling per order. OH add 7% tax.)

Send check or money order, no cash or C.O.D.s please.

Name _____

Address _____

City, State, Zip _____

To place a credit card order, call 1-800-847-8270.
Send to: Heartsong Presents Reader Service, PO Box 721, Uhrichsville, OH 44683

❤ ❤ ❤ ❤ ❤ ❤ ❤ ❤ ❤ ❤ ❤ ❤ ❤ ❤ ❤ ❤ ❤

Hearts♥ng

Any 12
Heartsong
Presents titles
for only
$27.00*

CONTEMPORARY ROMANCE IS CHEAPER BY THE DOZEN!

Buy any assortment of twelve *Heartsong Presents* titles and save 25% off of the already discounted price of $2.97 each!

*plus $2.00 shipping and handling per order and sales tax where applicable.

HEARTSONG PRESENTS TITLES AVAILABLE NOW:

___HP242 Far Above Rubies, B. Melby & C. Wienke
___HP245 Crossroads, T. and J. Peterson
___HP246 Brianna's Pardon, G. Clover
___HP261 Race of Love, M. Panagiotopoulos
___HP262 Heaven's Child, G. Fields
___HP265 Hearth of Fire, C. L. Reece
___HP278 Elizabeth's Choice, L. Lyle
___HP298 A Sense of Belonging, T. Fowler
___HP302 Seasons, G. G. Martin
___HP305 Call of the Mountain, Y. Lehman
___HP306 Piano Lessons, G. Sattler
___HP317 Love Remembered, A. Bell
___HP318 Born for This Love, B. Bancroft
___HP321 Fortress of Love, M. Panagiotopoulos
___HP322 Country Charm, D. Mills
___HP325 Gone Camping, G. Sattler
___HP326 A Tender Melody, B. L. Etchison
___HP329 Meet My Sister, Tess, K. Billerbeck
___HP330 Dreaming of Castles, G. G. Martin
___HP337 Ozark Sunrise, H. Alexander
___HP338 Somewhere a Rainbow, Y. Lehman
___HP341 It Only Takes a Spark, P. K. Tracy
___HP342 The Haven of Rest, A. Boeshaar
___HP349 Wild Tiger Wind, G. Buck
___HP350 Race for the Roses, L. Snelling
___HP353 Ice Castle, J. Livingston
___HP354 Finding Courtney, B. L. Etchison
___HP361 The Name Game, M. G. Chapman
___HP377 Come Home to My Heart, J. A. Grote
___HP378 The Landlord Takes a Bride, K. Billerbeck
___HP390 Love Abounds, A. Bell
___HP394 Equestrian Charm, D. Mills
___HP401 Castle in the Clouds, A. Boeshaar
___HP402 Secret Ballot, Y. Lehman
___HP405 The Wife Degree, A. Ford
___HP406 Almost Twins, G. Sattler
___HP409 A Living Soul, H. Alexander
___HP410 The Color of Love, D. Mills
___HP413 Remnant of Victory, J. Odell

___HP414 The Sea Beckons, B. L. Etchison
___HP417 From Russia with Love, C. Coble
___HP418 Yesteryear, G. Brandt
___HP421 Looking for a Miracle, W. E. Brunstetter
___HP422 Condo Mania, M. G. Chapman
___HP425 Mustering Courage, L. A. Coleman
___HP426 To the Extreme, T. Davis
___HP429 Love Ahoy, C. Coble
___HP430 Good Things Come, J. A. Ryan
___HP433 A Few Flowers, G. Sattler
___HP434 Family Circle, J. L. Barton
___HP438 Out in the Real World, K. Paul
___HP441 Cassidy's Charm, D. Mills
___HP442 Vision of Hope, M. H. Flinkman
___HP445 McMillian's Matchmakers, G. Sattler
___HP449 An Ostrich a Day, N. J. Farrier
___HP450 Love in Pursuit, D. Mills
___HP454 Grace in Action, K. Billerbeck
___HP458 The Candy Cane Calaboose, J. Spaeth
___HP461 Pride and Pumpernickel, A. Ford
___HP462 Secrets Within, G. G. Martin
___HP465 Talking for Two, W. E. Brunstetter
___HP466 Risa's Rainbow, A. Boeshaar
___HP469 Beacon of Truth, P. Griffin
___HP470 Carolina Pride, T. Fowler
___HP473 The Wedding's On, G. Sattler
___HP474 You Can't Buy Love, K. Y'Barbo
___HP477 Extreme Grace, T. Davis
___HP478 Plain and Fancy, W. E. Brunstetter
___HP481 Unexpected Delivery, C. M. Hake
___HP482 Hand Quilted with Love, J. Livingston
___HP485 Ring of Hope, B. L. Etchison
___HP486 The Hope Chest, W. E. Brunstetter
___HP489 Over Her Head, G. G. Martin
___HP490 A Class of Her Own, J. Thompson
___HP493 Her Home or Her Heart, K. Elaine
___HP494 Mended Wheels, A. Bell & J. Sagal
___HP497 Flames of Deceit, R. Dow & A. Snaden

(If ordering from this page, please remember to include it with the order form.)

Presents

__HP498 *Charade*, P. Humphrey
__HP501 *The Thrill of the Hunt*, T. H. Murray
__HP502 *Whole in One*, A. Ford
__HP505 *Happily Ever After*, M. Panagiotopoulos
__HP506 *Cords of Love*, L. A. Coleman
__HP509 *His Christmas Angel*, G. Sattler
__HP510 *Past the Ps Please*, Y. Lehman
__HP513 *Licorice Kisses*, D. Mills
__HP514 *Roger's Return*, M. Davis
__HP517 *The Neighborly Thing to Do*, W. E. Brunstetter
__HP518 *For a Father's Love*, J. A. Grote
__HP521 *Be My Valentine*, J. Livingston
__HP522 *Angel's Roost*, J. Spaeth
__HP525 *Game of Pretend*, J. Odell
__HP526 *In Search of Love*, C. Lynxwiler
__HP529 *Major League Dad*, K. Y'Barbo
__HP530 *Joe's Diner*, G. Sattler
__HP533 *On a Clear Day*, Y. Lehman
__HP534 *Term of Love*, M. Pittman Crane
__HP537 *Close Enough to Perfect*, T. Fowler
__HP538 *A Storybook Finish*, L. Bliss
__HP541 *The Summer Girl*, A. Boeshaar
__HP542 *Clowning Around*, W. E. Brunstetter
__HP545 *Love Is Patient*, C. M. Hake
__HP546 *Love Is Kind*, J. Livingston
__HP549 *Patchwork and Politics*, C. Lynxwiler
__HP550 *Woodhaven Acres*, B. Etchison
__HP553 *Bay Island*, B. Loughran

__HP554 *A Donut a Day*, G. Sattler
__HP557 *If You Please*, T. Davis
__HP558 *A Fairy Tale Romance*, M. Panagiotopoulos
__HP561 *Ton's Vow*, K. Cornelius
__HP562 *Family Ties*, J. L. Barton
__HP565 *An Unbreakable Hope*, K. Billerbeck
__HP566 *The Baby Quilt*, J. Livingston
__HP569 *Ageless Love*, L. Bliss
__HP570 *Beguiling Masquerade*, C. G. Page
__HP573 *In a Land Far Far Away*, M. Panagiotopoulos
__HP574 *Lambert's Pride*, L. A. Coleman and R. Hauck
__HP577 *Anita's Fortune*, K. Cornelius
__HP578 *The Birthday Wish*, J. Livingston
__HP581 *Love Online*, K. Billerbeck
__HP582 *The Long Ride Home*, A. Boeshaar
__HP585 *Compassion's Charm*, D. Mills
__HP586 *A Single Rose*, P. Griffin
__HP589 *Changing Seasons*, C. Reece and J. Reece-Demarco
__HP590 *Secret Admirer*, G. Sattler
__HP593 *Angel Incognito*, J. Thompson
__HP594 *Out on a Limb*, G. Gaymer Martin
__HP597 *Let My Heart Go*, B. Huston
__HP598 *More Than Friends*, T. Hancock Murray
__HP601 *Timing Is Everything*, T. V. Bateman
__HP602 *Dandelion Bride*, J. Livingston

Great Inspirational Romance at a Great Price!

Heartsong Presents books are inspirational romances in contemporary and historical settings, designed to give you an enjoyable, spirit-lifting reading experience. You can choose wonderfully written titles from some of today's best authors like Hannah Alexander, Andrea Boeshaar, Yvonne Lehman, Tracie Peterson, and many others.

When ordering quantities less than twelve, above titles are $2.97 each.
Not all titles may be available at time of order.

SEND TO: **Heartsong Presents** Reader's Service
P.O. Box 721, Uhrichsville, Ohio 44683

Please send me the items checked above. I am enclosing $ _____
(please add $2.00 to cover postage per order. OH add 7% tax. NJ add 6%.). Send check or money order, no cash or C.O.D.s, please.

To place a credit card order, call 1-800-847-8270.

NAME _____

ADDRESS _____

CITY/STATE _____ ZIP_____

HPS 10-04

*H*EARTSONG ❤ PRESENTS

Love Stories
Are Rated G!

That's for godly, gratifying, and of course, great! If you love a thrilling love story but don't appreciate the sordidness of some popular paperback romances, **Heartsong Presents** is for you. In fact, **Heartsong Presents** is the premiere inspirational romance book club featuring love stories where Christian faith is the primary ingredient in a marriage relationship.

Sign up today to receive your first set of four, never-before-published Christian romances. Send no money now; you will receive a bill with the first shipment. You may cancel at any time without obligation, and if you aren't completely satisfied with any selection, you may return the books for an immediate refund!

Imagine. . .four new romances every four weeks—two historical, two contemporary—with men and women like you who long to meet the one God has chosen as the love of their lives. . .all for the low price of $10.99 postpaid.

To join, simply complete the coupon below and mail to the address provided. **Heartsong Presents** romances are rated G for another reason: They'll arrive Godspeed!

YES! Sign me up for Hearts❤ng!

NEW MEMBERSHIPS WILL BE SHIPPED IMMEDIATELY!
Send no money now. We'll bill you only $10.99 postpaid with your first shipment of four books. Or for faster action, call toll free 1-800-847-8270.

NAME _____

ADDRESS _____

CITY_____ STATE_____ ZIP_____

MAIL TO: HEARTSONG PRESENTS, P.O. Box 721, Uhrichsville, Ohio 44683
or visit www.heartsongpresents.com